Praise for
A Summer to Treasure

A Summer to Treasure by Leslea Wahl is a fast-paced family adventure that people of all ages will enjoy reading. Siblings Celia, Luke, and Austin are wholesome, engaging siblings that one can't help but relate to on multiple levels. Throw in loving, concerned parents and a grandmother with secrets and a love for adventure, and you have the perfect mix of fun, friendship, building relationships, and creating lifetime bonds. As a big fan of our national parks, I enjoyed visiting many along the way. *A Summer to Treasure* is a must-read that you and your family will not want to miss!

-Andrea Jo Rodgers, author of *Heaven-Sent Miracles & Rescues* and *Saving Mount Rushmore, Mission One*

A must-read for teens, *A Summer to Treasure* is well-crafted story that offers hints of mystery, relatable and authentic characters, and a landscape of real-world destinations that readers will want to visit. It can seem like today's culture wants to systematically deconstruct and poison the thoughts and attitudes of teens about parents, siblings, and even the essential notion of "family" itself. But this story paints a refreshing portrait of the powerful value of family and reminds teens of the richness of multi-generational relationships. *A Summer to Treasure* is faith-honoring and virtue-rich book that is a truly fun summer—or anytime—read!

-Cathy Gilmore, author, founder, CEO, Virtue Literacy Project

Praise, continued

This is the thirteenth time I have read a book or published story from the pen of Leslea Wahl. I always love her characters and the ways she weaves both faith and mysteries into her stories. Wahl really brings to life the friendships, the family interactions, and the real struggles. The mystery in this work is a little more layered. The summer trip is to recreate a vacation the grandmother and her brother experienced 60 years earlier, as sort of a remake but with a surprising twist as the family learns a secret about Grandma.

The story is written in a series of first-person narratives, a style that Gordon Korman uses often, and it works so well with this book. Korman is known as a master of the "school story," and I would state Wahl is a master of the "vacation story." *A Summer to Treasure* also reminds me of Madeleine L'Engle's Chronos series. There is nothing supernatural or paranormal. It is real-time real-world fiction. Wahl does an amazing job writing about this family, their faith, their discoveries, and the rebuilding of their family bonds on this summer road trip.

-Steven McEvoy, writer and member of Catholic Writers Guild

A month on the road. A cramped camper. No cell service and siblings who refuse to get along. Amid groans and gripes begins a family vacation that promises to be a nightmare. But an undaunted grandmother and an unsolved mystery quickly turn the dreaded trip into a heart-pounding adventure, leaving the teen trio to discover not merely a long-lost treasure in the desert wilderness, but the even greater lost treasure of family closeness and compassion. An exciting, heartwarming summer read from a top-notch storyteller! Not to be missed!

-Susan Peek, author, *Saint Magnus: The Last Viking*

The Webbers' Summer Trip

A Summer to Treasure

Leslea Wahl

To JWahl, T-Rex, and Jaco.
Your supportive, caring relationship
is the inspiration for this novel.
May you always be the best of friends.
God bless.

Contents

Contents

Chapter 1

Celia:
Sucked Into the Black Hole

This couldn't be happening.

Celia stared at her parents. *Are they serious?* They generally weren't known for their senses of humor, but still she held out a thin sliver of hope that their shocking announcement was some sort of weird experiment. A let's-freak-out-the-kids-then-break-it-to-them-that-it's-a-joke sort of prank. But they showed no sign of moving past the life-altering pronouncement. Okay, maybe not *life*-altering, more like summer-destroying. Either way, she had to admit it, this beyond-awful plan would make the perfect, cruddy ending to her disastrous school year.

The moment Dad had suggested the five of them talk in the formal living room, her internal bad-news radar started pinging. Nothing good ever came from a family meeting. Her gaze shifted to her brothers to determine their take on the whole situation.

Luke's forearms flexed as he clasped his hands. Celia's older brother always got his way. Surely, he could use his smooth-talking skills to persuade Mom and Dad out of this horrendous idea. He may be a royal pain and too cool to give her the time of day lately, but she'd learned over the years that it was best to let him schmooze the folks with his calm nonsense before she went into full freak out mode. This insight had come from years of being sent to her room for shrill outbursts, only to find out—after her punishment—that Luke, with his steady voice of reason, had miraculously gotten them to arrive at her desired outcome. The guy really should go into politics. He already had the clean-cut, all-American look going for him. When it came to reading people, understanding what made them tick, and using it to get his way, her older sibling was a pro.

Luke's favorite-child status was beyond annoying, but hey, if he used it to her advantage, then have at it, big bro. Take the lead.

He must've felt her desperate gaze given the annoyed look he shot her way before turning his attention to the folks. Celia wasn't sure if his grumpiness was aimed at her for staring, or at their folks for the bombshell announcement. Hopefully, the latter.

Luke's Adam's apple bobbed as he swallowed. "Umm. So, you're thinking we should spend our summer vacation driving around the country in an RV with Grandma?"

Celia's skin crawled when Luke gave voice to the stupid idea. Road tripping in some lame camper with her parents, brothers, and *grandmother?*

Um . . . don't think so. Come on, Luke, help a girl out. Time for his persuasive superpowers.

Dad clenched his jaw. "Yep. That is the plan."

Luke rubbed the back of his neck. "Wow. That does sound fun. Are you talking like a weekend trip or something?"

Mom shook her head, her dyed-blonde bob swayed with the movement. "No. It would be a bit longer than that." She nudged Dad with her knee.

The slight movement set Celia further on edge. *This can't be good.*

Dad ran a hand through his brown hair. A few gray strands flecked the boring shade that he'd passed on to his children. "We would be gone for a month. Or so."

"A month! No way! Not happening! *Ever!* I have plans for the summer." Celia couldn't stop the screech—it just flew right out of her mouth.

"Celia! That's enough."

You'd think she were five, the way Mom scolded her. Celia threw her head back against the couch cushion.

Luke pierced her with another scorching glance. This time she knew without a doubt who was the intended target. She bit the inside of her cheek to prevent any further outbursts.

Turning back to their parents, her older brother leaned forward, elbows resting on his knees. "I'm sure we could see a lot of cool things in a month. Can you get away from work for that long?"

Oh, good point! Why hadn't she thought of that?

Dad clasped his hands together. "Well, I have a lot of vacation time built up, so I arranged to work part-time on my laptop. You all sleep later than me, anyway. I can get a couple hours in each morning."

What? Come on, Luke, you gotta do better than that!

A flash of surprise flickered across her brother's face. "Oh, that's cool! Hey, sorry to be the one to put the kibosh on this plan, but I'm not sure I can get away for that long. Football pre-season starts up in mid-June, and you know how Coach is about missing practices—especially the seniors. I don't want to mess up my chance of being named one of the captains this season. Besides, I was planning on working a lot this summer."

He deftly ignored the other reason he wouldn't want to be gone for so long. Jenna. His clingy girlfriend could never survive without him for a month. Celia's quick glance at Austin to gauge his reaction only raised her frustration level. Her younger brother was slouched behind a pillow, eyes aimed at his lap—no doubt playing a game on his phone. The twerp couldn't even pay attention long enough to stay focused during one family meeting. Typical.

One swift kick to his foot made him jump, shaggy brown hair flopping over his eyes.

"Huh?" He brushed the messy mop out of his way.

She shot him a withering glare, which produced the desired result of him abandoning his phone, at least for a moment.

Luke motioned toward Austin. "Traveling that long would also cheat Austin out of summer camp. He's going into eighth grade. This is his last chance to attend. And Celia would miss . . ." His gaze flicked her way. "Whatever it is that Celia does."

Seriously? He couldn't come up with anything better than that? Unbelievable. He could take all the time in the world to understand everyone else, but his own sister? Forget it. Now that he was about to be a senior, his ego had ticked up a notch, from obnoxious to unbearable. She resisted the tempting urge of telling him off. Right now, though, it was more important that he be the voice of reason to Mom and Dad.

Dad ran his hand along his jawline. Sunshine streamed through the kitchen window and gleamed off his wedding band. The weather outside in direct contrast to the dreariness that had suddenly infiltrated their home. "Look. I know this is not how any of you wanted to spend your summer. Honestly, it wouldn't be my first choice, either. But we're doing this for Grandma."

Mom turned on the spousal support and rubbed Dad's back. "That's right. As you may have noticed, Grandma hasn't really been herself since her trip to visit her brother."

Grandma had always been close to her only brother, Harry. Over the years, she'd shared numerous stories about him, causing Celia to think how lucky her grandmother was to have only one male sibling to deal with. He was a monk in some tiny town in Kansas, so they didn't see each other too often.

Now that Celia thought about it—Mom was right. Grandma hadn't been her upbeat self since she'd gotten back from that trip. Last weekend, when she'd been over for a barbeque, she'd been totally distracted. Grandma usually made family dinners much less stressful with her knack of including everyone in the conversation and relaying funny stories about the folks at her senior living complex. Celia hadn't really thought anything of it until now, since she'd had more pressing matters on her mind.

"Is everything all right with her?" Luke's forehead scrunched with concern.

Dad's shoulder raised in a half-shrug. "Honestly, I don't know. She says everything's fine, but she's certainly not herself. I'm worried that maybe . . ." He shook his head then glanced toward Mom.

Mom cleared her throat, rescuing him from whatever he was about to say. "Apparently, Grandma wants to relive a vacation she and her brother took as kids with their parents. They spent several weeks driving through the Southwest visiting national parks." Her face hardened with determination as she took in her children's matching are-you-kidding-me expressions.

This was ridiculous. How would making the rest of them completely miserable help Grandma feel better?

Dad leaned forward. "We don't know why she's so insistent on doing this. In fact, we also pushed back on the idea, but she wouldn't drop it." He reached over and grabbed Mom's hand. "After much discussion, we decided that maybe this is a needed wake-up call. Grandma won't be with us forever." His voice caught with emotion. Mom's hand tightened around his, giving him strength to continue. "Each year we have her is a blessing."

Austin's eyes widened. "Wait. Is something wrong with her?"

The gaze between Mom and Dad lingered for a moment before he shook his head no. "She claims that she and Harry were going through some items from their childhood and began reminiscing about their special trip out west. She insists that she's fine but, because she's getting older, thinks this could be the last big trip she can take, and she wants all of us to go with her."

Celia exchanged glances with her brothers, then swallowed her frustration. They'd all seen the extended look between their parents. Even Luke's smooth talk wouldn't get them out of this one. Something was going on, and none of them could possibly say no to Grandma's request. But a month in an enclosed space with the family? Pure torture.

Chapter 2

LUKE:
ROLL WITH THE PUNCHES

Jenna encircled Luke with her thin arms. He tried not to flinch or pull away, but the PDA in front of his family made him uncomfortable.

"I'm going to miss you terribly." The emotional strain in his girlfriend's voice filled him with guilt. *Don't be a jerk. She's going to miss you. Man up.*

So, instead of squirming out of her embrace, Luke pulled her close, breathing in the scent of her floral shampoo. "I know. I wish I didn't have to go." Since they'd started dating in the fall, they'd seen each other almost every day. Being apart for a whole month would be tough. "At least we can text and send photos."

Celia brushed past them on her way to the motorhome Dad had rented for their insanely long trip. Luke ignored the shake of his sister's head. Celia never even tried to hide the fact that she was no fan of Jenna. Granted, she didn't seem to be a fan of anything anymore. No, that wasn't true. There were a few things she enjoyed, such as sulking around, listening to music through her earbuds, and doodling in a stupid sketchbook.

He'd pretty much given up trying to figure out what was up with his sister. In the fall, things had seemed fine. Her freshman year began with her hanging out with all her middle school friends, but then something changed. She went from zero to weird in a millisecond and began infiltrating the fringe crowd. Luckily, no one at school made a big deal of his sister's aversion-to-color grunge phase.

"Thanks for coming by to see us off, Jenna." Dad's diplomatic words were clearly meant to end this good-bye scene. For once, Luke welcomed the disruption since he had no clue how to extricate himself from Jenna on his own without setting off the minefield of her emotions.

She pulled away and wiped her tears. "Of course. I couldn't let Luke leave without a proper send-off."

"Come on, gang. Let's hit the road," Dad hollered. He then leaned close to Jenna like he was about to reveal a big secret. "The beauty of traveling in a motorhome is that we don't need a million bathroom breaks."

"Siena, come!" Austin squatted down, and their goldendoodle cautiously shimmied up to him, heavy panting a sure indicator of her nerves.

"Oh . . ." Jenna reached down to pat Siena's soft head. "She doesn't want to leave, either."

Austin shook his head. "She loves car rides. Once we get moving, she'll be fine. She just gets worried when we start packing. I guess she thinks we'll drop her off at the kennel." He stroked Siena's back. "Don't worry, girl. This time you get to come along." The dog answered with a lick across his cheek.

Mom locked the front door of the house, then joined them in front of their home-on-wheels for the next month. "Okay. I turned off the water and set the alarm. I think we're all set."

"Good." Dad motioned toward the RV. "Pile in, everyone. Let's be on our way."

"Wait!" Grandma's head popped out of the motorhome window. Her wavy gray hair framed her smiling face.

Now what?

"We need a photo to commemorate the start of our journey." Grandma pointed at Jenna. "Will you take a photo of us, dear?"

"Sure."

Luke handed Jenna his phone, then waited patiently with the rest of the family while Celia slowly plodded out of the camper, her annoyance on full display. Hopefully, she wouldn't ruin the picture with her usual scowl.

After posing for a few shots, Luke pulled his girl-friend in for one last hug as the monstrous vehicle roared to life. His cue to leave. He smiled for a few more insisted-upon selfies, then climbed into the motorhome with the rest of the family.

He scanned the space. While he'd been being a good boyfriend, everyone else had staked out their spots. Dad manned the driver's seat, with Mom next to him assuming the role of co-pilot, a tail-wagging Siena perched between them, her front paws draped over the console. Celia and Austin had commandeered the two bolted-in-place swivel lounge chairs. Both hovered over their phones, Celia listening to something through earbuds, tapping her foot to some unknown song, and Austin already lost to his game du jour.

That left only one open seat—next to Grandma on the L-shaped bench at the table. Since the matriarch of the family had already chosen the short end, the seat with a direct line of sight to the front window, he plopped next to her on the bench that ran under the long window.

Outside, Jenna waved frantically to get his attention, then blew a series of kisses. He smiled and waved, touched by her emotional, although slightly over-the-top, farewell. Even though a casual observer might assume he were being deployed, not heading off for a family vacation—he found it sweet.

The mammoth camper lurched away from the curb, convulsing down the street as Dad grew accustomed to the touchy pedals.

"We're off on our adventure!" Dad honked the horn to emphasize the moment.

Luke squeezed his eyes shut. *This is going to be the longest month ever.*

The RV had barely made it out of their Colorado Springs neighborhood when his first text from Jenna came through.

I miss you already.

Luke grinned at the message. It'd only been six minutes since her tearful farewell. Grateful for the distraction from Dad's choice of road-trip music (who would want to relive the '80s?), he typed a quick reply to Jenna.

Setting his phone down, he glanced at Celia, her head swaying to the beat of her music. She had the right idea. If only he knew where he'd stashed his earbuds.

"Did Jenna send you a message already?"

He looked toward Grandma's smile. "Uh, yeah. She's going to have a tough time while I'm on this trip. We've only ever gone a few days without seeing each other." The phone buzzed with Jenna's reply.

Grandma pushed away the leather notebook in front of her. "Have you ever heard the saying 'Absence makes the heart grow fonder'?"

Luke shook his head. "Don't think so."

She nodded toward his phone. "A little time and distance can be wonderful for a relationship."

"Oh, yeah?" Jenna's newest message informed him that she'd already posted one of their goodbye selfies. He typed a quick reply.

"Did you know that your grandpa was in the military while we were dating? He was deployed, and we didn't see each other for a whole year."

"Really?" His phone buzzed again, but he forced himself to keep his focus on his grandmother. "A whole year? That must've been rough." Grandma was pretty tough, most likely she'd showed a lot less emotion than Jenna, even when her guy went off to war and not a simple road trip.

The skin around Grandma's eyes crinkled with a smile. "It was. And we didn't have texting or computers back then to help us keep in touch."

Hard to even imagine. "Were you able to call each other?"

She shook her head. "Believe it or not, it was too expensive. We wrote letters."

"Oh, wow. That must've taken a while to hear from each other." No instantaneous messages a hundred times a day. *What did they do with all their free time?*

A faraway look turned her eyes hazy. "I cherished his letters." She focused on her oldest grandson. "I bet Jenna would love to receive a letter from you."

"A letter? What would I write?" He pictured Jenna's confused face at getting a letter in the mail.

"Well, what do you type to her now?"

"I don't know. Nothing important."

"You could tell her about all that we see on our trip. And you could open up your heart and share your feelings." Her smile turned into a mischievous grin. "Girls like that sort of thing."

He shifted in his seat, glancing away. *Open up my heart? Like in some dumb romantic comedy? Don't think so.* "I'm not sure. I don't think I'd have enough to say to write a whole letter."

"Maybe a postcard then. You could send her one from each of our stops. That's what I'm planning to do; send postcards to update Harry on the trip." She grinned. "In fact, I bought a Pike's Peak postcard the other day so I can let him know we started our excursion."

Hmm. Postcards? Not a bad idea. That he could handle. "She might actually like that." If there was one thing he knew about Jenna, it was her weakness for rom-coms.

He glanced at Jenna's newest query—wondering how far from home they'd driven. He peered out the window. Not far. And at their current speed, they might never reach the first destination. When semis zoom past, you know you're in for a long journey. He quickly answered the text, then stuffed the phone in his pocket. Enough for now.

He returned his attention to Grandma. "So, Dad said this trip is kind of recreating one you took as a kid?"

"Yes. Want to hear the story?" Her face beamed, obviously anxious for a trip down memory lane.

"Yeah, sure." Maybe she'd reveal what was really going on.

Before she could begin, Luke snatched two pillows from the bench and flung them at his siblings.

Austin glanced around for whatever he'd missed. Celia pulled out one earbud with an all-too-familiar scowl.

"Hey, enough with the phones. Grandma wants to tell us about the trip to the Southwest she took as a kid."

His siblings dutifully put their devices away, and all three turned their attention to their beloved grandmother.

"Well." The elderly woman rested her hands on the table. "I don't know if you know this or not, but my father was a professor of archeology."

"Cool! Like Indiana Jones?" Austin blurted out. "I loved that ride at Disneyland."

Grandma's gaze flicked off to the left as her face warmed with a smile. "Well, we did have some interesting adventures."

Huh. How have we never heard this before?

Grandma peered out the window before continuing. "He didn't teach summer classes, so every year, when school ended, we took a family trip. One year, we explored the Great Lakes. Another year, we ventured to Alaska. But my favorite trip was when we visited the national parks in the Southwest."

"Really?" Austin's face scrunched up. "Better than Alaska?"

Celia punched his arm. "Let her speak."

Grandma smiled at Austin, deftly ignoring Celia like they all longed to do. "Well, Alaska was special, too. But I think I enjoyed our trip to Arizona and Utah so much because Harry and I were old enough to explore a little without supervision, but we weren't too old to pretend and create our own adventures."

"How old were you?" Celia actually looked interested in something besides her sketchpad.

Weird.

"I think I was probably about ten, so Harry would have been twelve."

"You were two years apart like we all are." Austin brushed a strand of unruly hair away from his eyes.

Grandma nodded. "Yep."

"Did your mother go along too?"

Luke shook his head. When not immersed in a video game, his little brother couldn't stop talking. Hopefully, he wouldn't be breaking out the annoying puns anytime soon.

"Yes. She was an artist and would spend hours at each location sketching or painting, trying to capture the beauty of the landscape."

Celia sat a little straighter. "Are all those paintings at your apartment hers?"

Grandma's eyebrows arched like she was surprised Celia had noticed the artwork. "They sure are. I always thought she was very talented. She sold a few, but I think she had more fun creating than selling them. But as you can imagine, with my father doing fieldwork and my mother painting, it left Harry and me with a lot of free time."

"That sounds like a great childhood." Although, they'd miss out on all the organized sports camps and stuff.

"It was." That faraway look flooded her eyes again.

"Did your visit with Harry bring back all those memories?" Luke probed, still hoping to discover more about the reason for the trip.

Grandma focused her gaze on him. "Yes. In fact, we'd both forgotten so much from those years." She took a moment to look each of her grandchildren in the eye. "I'm not sure if you're all aware, but Harry and I lost our parents when we were in our twenties. They died in an accident—during one of their summer excursions."

Celia let out a little gasp. "How sad."

Grandma nodded. "Yes, it was very tragic. I suppose it was difficult to think about those trips after they'd passed away."

Luke's curiosity piqued. "So, why the sudden interest in recreating one then?"

Her mouth curved up into a small smile. "I'm glad you asked. When they died, I was a new bride. Charlie and I lived in a small house. Harry was discerning religious life. Neither of us had the room to store any of our parents' belongings, so our uncle kept several boxes for us." She folded her hands in front of her. "I'm not sure why, maybe it was just too painful, but neither of us ever retrieved those items. A few months ago, a cousin contacted us to let us know their family home is being sold, and he wondered if we wanted the boxes or if he should just throw them away. Harry and I decided we should finally face the past and go through them."

"That's what you did during your recent visit?" Austin pushed a wayward strand of hair out of his face.

Grandma's smile turned wistful. "Yes. And it was wonderful. We had such a good time reliving so many fond memories. There were notebooks with our mother's sketches, old photographs, our father's journals, and even the diary my mother had given me for our Southwest trip." She patted the notebook next to her.

Celia's mouth dropped open. "That's from when you were ten?"

Grandma ran her hand along the smooth leather. "Yes. It's been so fun to read through the entries." She closed her eyes for a moment before continuing. "It made me so sad that we'd forgotten how special our family trips were—like we'd dishonored our parents' memories. Those summers are truly some of my most cherished moments of my life, and I really want to share at least one of them with you."

Speechless, Luke glanced at his siblings. Celia seemed to be holding back tears as she bit her lip, while Austin squirmed uncomfortably in his chair. Obviously, they were both at a loss for words as well.

"Umm . . . so, what's our first stop on this trip?" Austin, of course, was the first to break the heavy silence.

"Check your phone." Luke knew his tone was harsher than the occasion called for, but seriously . . . could the kid be any more incompetent? "Dad texted us all an agenda."

"You told me to put my phone away." There was no missing the "so there" look he aimed at Luke.

"He's got a point." Celia smirked, then reached out her hand to high-five Austin.

"We aren't traveling too far today." Grandma's response prevented Luke from launching a comeback.

The chances of surviving a month in this motorized prison with his siblings was practically zero. But he'd have to try—for Grandma's sake.

"We're camping near the Great Sand Dunes tonight," Grandma patiently shared. "Tomorrow, we'll see how far you can hike on them."

Austin's eyes bulged. "Sand dunes? In Colorado? No way!"

"You haven't been there before?" Grandma's forehead creased.

"We were there when I was, like, in third grade," Luke explained. "Austin probably doesn't remember it."

"Figures," Austin pouted. "They did all the fun stuff when I was too little to remember." He reached for his phone.

Grandma patted the table before the kid could disappear into his cyberworld. "Do you all want to play cards?"

Luke grinned. "Absolutely." Not only was she offering a distraction from the '80s rock anthems and the RV's painfully slow pace, but Grandma had revealed the reason for the trip and was now back to her game-playing self. All was right in the world.

Grandma

Dear Harry,

I'm so thankful I was able to convince them to take this trip. We are now on our way, and the stage is set. Please pray we can accomplish our goal. I will keep you posted.

Your loving sister,

Grace

Chapter 3

Austin:
Interface

"Do you think Grandma is dying?" Austin hadn't planned to blurt it out, but the thought wouldn't stop ricocheting around his brain.

Celia glanced over her shoulder. "Why would you ask such a thing?"

Unable to continue his forward momentum up the mountain of sand the three siblings were climbing, Austin stopped to catch his breath. He shifted the rope of the sled he was pulling to the opposite hand. *Who would have guessed it's so hard to walk through sand? Camels make it look easy.* "I dunno. I'm not sure I buy her explanation about the trip. She could have just shared pictures and told us about her childhood adventures. But instead, she suddenly wants to spend all this extra time with us? Something just seems off. And besides, she's always reading her Bible." Thankfully, his siblings stopped the uphill trek as well.

Luke wiped the sweat from his forehead. "She's always read her Bible a lot. But you have a point. I wonder why she was so adamant about the trip. It's not like when she suggested it Dad thought it sounded like a great idea. She really had to push for it—which isn't like her." He uncapped his water and took a long swig.

Celia lifted the hair off the back of her neck. "Yeah, you're right. She's the most chill person I know."

Austin shivered as a wave of fear rippled through him. "So, you think it's true? She's dying?" They weren't supposed to agree with him.

Luke shook his head. "No. Don't you think Mom and Dad would tell us that?"

"Maybe if we spend time with her and get her talking, we'll figure out her real motive." Celia started trekking up the hill once again. "Come on, losers."

Geez, where'd she get her energy? Celia was the perfect-grades sibling, not the athletic one. Big brother had that covered. "What's your hurry? Someplace you need to be?"

"Yeah, anywhere away from you."

Just the set-up Austin needed. "You know, Celia, sometimes you can be nice, but right now you're being a total *sand witch*. Get it? Sandwich?" He grinned at his pun.

Celia's forward momentum didn't even slow. "Hilarious."

"I think you mean *hill-arious.*" Austin stared past her to the top of the mountain of sand they were traversing, then back to where they started. *Ugh.* Only halfway to the top of this first dune.

"Come on." Luke nudged him. "We can't let her beat us."

"Why is there so much sand in the middle of a mountain range?" With a sigh, Austin adjusted the sled again and plowed forward. Sliding down the huge dune better be as fun as it sounded. "I don't get it. Where'd it come from?"

"How should I know?" Luke asked. "Guess you should read the brochure the park ranger gave us."

Austin continued his slow, stalwart march. With each step, his foot sank into the sand, then had to be pulled out. He could build an entire castle and surrounding village with the amount of grit in his shoes. Maybe Grandma had the right idea, waiting at the bottom with Siena. He and his siblings had declined the offer to join their parents on a smaller dune, thinking they knew better. He hated to admit that the boring adult choices now sounded much more appealing. Austin's aching legs screamed in protest, but somewhere deep inside, determination kicked in. If Luke and Celia could make it, he could too.

As they slowly neared the summit, Luke passed by with a few long strides. Show off. By the time Austin and Celia caught up, Luke stood enjoying the view.

Austin bent over, hands on his knees, sucking in gulps of air.

"Whew!" Celia leaned on his back to steady herself.

Luke chuckled. "You two really need to get in shape."

Here it comes—Luke's usual rant about what slugs we are and that we should join some sport. Mr. Football's mind was so full of himself, it never occurred to him that some people might not like sports.

Celia huffed out a breath. *Good, no need to say a thing.* Austin grinned, ready to enjoy the fireworks while she told Luke off for the both of them.

"Maybe you're right."

What? Austin tilted his head to look at the girl who seemed to have mistaken him for a leaning post. Surely, it was some imposter. A possible shapeshifter in their midst. Because clearly, it was not Celia. When the doppelganger removed her elbow from his back, he straightened.

"Whoa." The view before them made him forget everything. Massive sand dunes stretched for miles, ending at towering mountains.

The siblings stood in silence for a few moments before Celia shivered. "Wouldn't it be horrible to be lost out there?"

"Couldn't happen." Luke snapped a photo with his phone. "Your footprints would be easy to follow."

Rookie mistake. Austin shook his head. "One quick windstorm would make footprints obsolete. But don't worry, a drone could easily find you. You'd just better hope it'd be a search-and-rescue drone and not a bomb-dropping one."

Celia laughed. "Why are you so weird?"

Austin grinned, unable to look away from his sister. He hadn't seen her happy in forever. He'd even pondered if she was still capable of smiling, like maybe her facial muscles were no longer upwardly mobile. She turned and caught him watching her. He flinched, anticipating the punch or slew of insults that were sure to come his way. But oddly, her smile widened. Bizarre. Maybe he was onto something with the whole imposter thing.

Luke held up his phone. "Selfie time."

Austin's head snapped toward his older brother. What was with these two? Oxygen deprivation? "You hate selfies."

"Not when we're somewhere like this. Come on. We need to capture the moment."

They leaned together, and Luke lifted the phone, making sure the sea of sand behind them was visible. Why couldn't it always be this way when they hung out? Of course, there really hadn't been any hanging out lately. Austin had become quite used to the old glare-and-brush-off routine from his siblings. Could this trip possibly change that? Doubtful.

Luke stuffed his phone in his pocket. "Okay, let's do this thing."

Celia set down her sled. "Ready."

Austin's sled landed next to hers. "Fine and *sandy.*"

Luke groaned at the joke, then plopped down his sled before taking a few steps back. "On the count of three." He rotated his baseball hat backward. "Three."

"Two." Austin took a deep breath.

Celia leaned forward. "One!"

Together, they ran forward then leapt onto their sleds and plummeted down the steep dune of sand.

The wind whipped through Austin's hair, the breeze a welcome relief from the blistering heat. "Woohoo!" *This sand sledding actually works!*

Celia shrieked as she flew past him. Luke joined with a hoot.

Not to be outdone by the kids' screams, Siena's excited barks echoed through the valley. Grandma joined in by cheering and waving her sun visor as they soared toward her. She looked like Grandma always looked—not sick at all. Maybe she really did just want to recreate her favorite trip. Hopefully.

Too soon, the sleds slowed to a stop. Siena sprinted toward them.

"That looked amazing!" Grandma set her purple visor back on top of her wavy hair, which appeared silver in the bright sunlight.

"It was!" Austin glanced at Celia and Luke. He bit his lip. Should he ask? He hated to ruin the moment with his knack for annoying them. *Ah, what the heck. They were bound to get annoyed sooner or later anyway.* "Want to go again?"

"Oh yeah!" Luke called.

Celia scrambled off her sled. "Race you to the top!"

Pure awesomeness.

Chapter 4

Celia:
Gray and Gloomy

The continuous pelting of rain against the camper added a new beat to the country song playing on the radio.
While Celia wasn't a fan of Luke's choice of tunes, it
was a welcome change from the '80s trash Dad liked
so much.

"I wish we could have a campfire." Austin's whine
sent a spasm of annoyance down her spine.

*And I wish I didn't have to sit here pretending to
have fun. Welcome to the real world, little brother,
where dreams don't come true.*

Dad shuffled the deck of cards they'd been using
to keep themselves amused for the last hour. "Don't

worry, we'll have plenty of time on this trip for fires and s'mores."

Celia massaged her temple, trying to keep the looming headache at bay. She was already tired of being stuck in the confined space with everyone—and it was only the second night. Surviving the month might prove literally impossible.

She longed to excuse herself, grab her earbuds, and escape to her bed with some decent music. Surprisingly, the top mattress of the bunkbed she and Grandma shared was quite comfortable. Although, their "bedroom" was really just a tiny nook strategically located across from the bathroom. *Whoever designs these rigs must love puzzles.* Despite the fun at the dunes, she was ready for some alone time. However, ending the family game night would certainly not go over well.

"Want to play another round?" Even Mom, the family cheerleader, looked bored.

Luke stretched his arms toward the ceiling. "Yeah, I guess. Not much else to do."

"Unless you're getting tired, Mom." Dad's concerned gaze flicked toward his mother. "We could call it a night."

"No. I'm fine." Grandma turned toward Celia and rolled her eyes.

To cover her amusement, Celia bowed her head and covered her mouth with her hand. *Oh, Grandma, I understand completely.* Dad's overprotectiveness could drive anyone crazy.

Mom stood and took the required two steps to reach the kitchenette. "Let's have some dessert. I brought brownies along."

Austin rubbed his hands together. "Now you're talkin'."

"I have an idea . . . something we can do while we eat our dessert," Grandma said.

"Sure, what do you have in mind?" Dad stuffed the cards back into their box.

"Why don't we tell stories about ourselves? Some incident that the rest of the family might not know about. Everyone can take a turn during our trip. I'll go first."

Celia squeezed her eyes shut. What kind of horrible idea was that? *Grandma, I thought we were on the same wavelength. Kindred spirits. Oh, how you disappoint me.*

"Sounds cool." Luke reached for the plate Mom handed him.

Oh sure, cool for him. He'd probably brag about some fabulous athletic accomplishment. And Austin would most likely share something stupid about a video game. With any luck, everyone would soon forget this idea. Because there was a reason her family didn't know the things they didn't know about her. Some things were personal and private—and should stay that way.

"Is there a story about you that we haven't heard yet?" Mom set a plate in front of Grandma.

"I have lots of stories. You don't know everything about me." Grandma gave a coy little smile as she savored a bite of her brownie, then glanced around the table. "My story is about the night your grandpa and I met."

Austin flicked a chunk of hair out of his eyes. "We know that one. You met at a church picnic, right?"

"Sort of." The family matriarch's mischievous smile added a bit of intrigue to the moment. The rest of the family shared questioning glances with one another.

"Well, you've piqued my curiosity," Dad admitted.

Grandma rested one hand on top of the other. "It was the day of the annual parish picnic. I was sixteen and hoping to team up with Walter Murphy for the three-legged race."

"Who?" Austin asked.

"He was this very cute boy that I had a crush on. I was determined to get him to notice me."

Celia's fork stopped halfway to her mouth. She'd never thought about her grandmother having a crush on someone. So weird.

"So, if you were crushing on this Walter guy, how'd you meet Grandpa?" Luke teased.

"I told you that you didn't know all my stories." Grandma smiled, suddenly looking much younger. "There I was, at the picnic waiting for Walter to show up. As families kept arriving, I stayed perched on a picnic bench, watching for him. Finally, my friend Julia convinced me to stop pining away and join the activities. Reluctantly, I let her drag me to the field where they were setting up for the three-legged race. I was so disappointed that Walter was not there to be my partner. My plan was ruined. But before I could feel too sorry for myself, there was a commotion behind us. Julia and I turned toward the woods to see who was yelling. Suddenly, two boys sprinted through the trees. Unfortunately, they were looking over their shoulders and plowed right into us."

She stopped to take another bite of her dessert, leaving everyone hanging. The siblings all looked toward Dad, but his blank face revealed that he'd never heard the story before either. Grandma swallowed her bite, then took a sip of water. A country crooner filled the silence as they waited for her dramatic pause to end.

The elderly woman set down her glass. "There we were, the four of us, sprawled across the ground, but the yelling from the woods didn't stop. I was about to tell the scruffy young man who had run into me a thing or two about watching where he was going, but I didn't have a chance. He grabbed my hand, yanked me up, and pulled me over to where couples were lining up for the three-legged race. I threw my hands to my hips and asked him what he thought he was doing. He grinned and said, 'Getting out of Ole' Man Franklin's line of sight.'"

She paused for another sip of water.

Celia leaned forward, picturing the whole scene: Grandma and her sassiness, the boy who resembled Huckleberry Finn in her mind, and the confused crowd. "Then what happened?"

Grandma pulled in a breath, her eyes glimmering. "I stared at this young man. He was such a mess—ripped jeans, covered in dirt. I recognized him as one of the boys my daddy always warned me about—a rough group from the other side of town. So, I had no intention of spending another moment with him, but then my eyes fell on Walter, who had finally arrived and was being rather friendly with Anna Mary Hathaway." Her chuckle made Celia smile. "I was so mad that all reason flew out of my head. I tied my ankle to that filthy young man's, ready to partner up with him just to spite Walter. As the sound of the starting gun sounded, Mr. Franklin came barreling through the woods, waving his shotgun and screaming obscenities. I grabbed the young man's hand, and we started running across the field. Most everyone else screamed and dove for cover, while a few men helped deal with Mr. Franklin, who kept bellowing about a gang of boys who stole something from him. As we crossed the finish line—in first place, I might add—we lost our balance and fell to the ground. I looked over at my unexpected partner and found myself peering into the most mesmerizing eyes I had ever seen."

"Was the scruffy guy Grandpa?"

Celia shot her younger brother a scathing glance that made him flinch.

Does he really think the cute guy could be someone besides Grandpa?

Dad's mouth fell open. "Dad was part of a gang? I never heard that before."

Celia didn't remember her grandfather very well. He'd passed away years before, but from what she'd heard, he was an honest, honorable, straight-laced man. In fact, he had been a judge.

Grandma's head tilted to the side. "Well, that's what people thought. Charlie and his friends were all very poor and lived on the side of town we were encouraged to avoid. But those boys weren't all bad. They were just trying to survive. Sadly, not all of them made it out of that poverty, but my Charlie did." Her face beamed with pride.

"Did he actually *steal* something?" Mom's wide eyes showed her surprise.

Grandma shrugged. "I suppose, technically. But you see, Mr. Franklin was the meanest man in town. He was usually drunk and treated everyone horribly. Anyone walking past his property could always hear him cursing at his animals, especially his poor dog."

"Oh . . . poor puppy." Celia reached a hand down to the dog curled at her feet and stroked Siena's soft, golden back.

"Well, that day, my sweet Charlie and his friends were walking past the Franklin house and saw him kick the dog. They devised a plan for two of them to cause a distraction while the other two rescued the animal. I was a dog lover, so I thought it was the sweetest thing I'd ever heard." She leaned back in her seat. "And that was it—I was in love and never gave Walter Murphy another thought. That was also the day I first learned that God has a plan for each of us—one that is often different than what we think we want. But His plan is always far better than ours could ever be."

No one spoke for a moment while Celia thought about her grandmother's words. *God has a plan for each of us.* While a nice inspirational saying, she wasn't sure she believed it.

"Was Grandpa arrested?" Austin broke the silence.

"More importantly, what happened to the dog?" Celia knew Grandpa ended up fine. But what about the poor, defenseless canine?

Grandma smiled at Austin. "Mr. Franklin tried to convince everyone that Charlie and his friends had stolen his dog, but there was no proof. The sheriff had gotten complaints from various people for years about Mr. Franklin's abusive behavior, so I don't think he was keen on pursuing the situation." She placed her wrinkled hand over Celia's. "As for the dog, one of the boys took it to live on a farm in a neighboring town. I heard he had a long, happy life with a loving family."

Thank goodness for the happy ending.

"And your father let you start dating this questionable boy?" Poor Dad still looked shocked to discover this new information about his own father.

Grandma chuckled. "Let me put it this way, proving his innocence to the sheriff was a whole lot easier than proving his worth to my daddy."

Mom gathered the empty dessert plates. "How come we never heard that story before?"

Grandma's bony shoulder rose in a shrug. "Charlie thought it was too scandalous for a judge to have such a background."

Maybe this story-sharing proposal of hers wasn't completely lame after all. But the likelihood of anyone else in the family having anything remotely interesting to share remained pretty slim.

Chapter 5

LUKE:
FULL COURT PRESS

Luke leaned in as close as he could to the roped-off staircase. There had to be a logical explanation for this structure. Sure, he believed in the miracles written in the Bible, but nowadays, mysterious phenomena had scientific explanations—right? Yet the tour guide claimed there were none. Was this simply a tourist trap or the actual scene of a divine occurrence? He glanced around to gauge his family's reactions, but none of them remained in the sanctuary. Whatever this was, it apparently didn't captivate them as much as it did him.

His gaze lingered one last time at the beautiful spiral staircase winding up to the choir loft. Maybe if he stared long enough, he could soak in the memory. He didn't know if it was its unusual story or the perfect curve of the wood, spiraling upwards, but something about it left him feeling awestruck. So, whether it was a miracle or not, he didn't want to ever forget this moment. When a large group of tourists pushed past him to gawk at the amazing structure, he decided it was his cue to catch up with his family in the gift shop.

After last night's storm, they'd woken to beautiful weather for the drive to New Mexico. Now they were in Santa Fe, where Grandma had insisted the Loretto Chapel needed to be their first stop.

Distracted, Luke leaned against a glass counter while the rest of the family browsed the vast array of souvenirs.

"What did you think of the staircase?" Grandma glanced at him as she handed a few postcards to the lady behind the counter.

"Do you really think Saint Joseph appeared and built that staircase for the nuns?" Saying the words out loud made the theory sound even more unbelievable. But what about all the unexplained facts surrounding the masterpiece?

Grandma touched the cross she always wore around her neck. What a dumb question. Of course, his devout grandmother believed the divine explanation. She gave him a warm smile as her fingers traced the delicate details of the necklace. "You are not alone with your query. The miraculous staircase has puzzled people for over a hundred years."

He stuffed his hands into his pockets. "It's weird that no one can figure out how it's built or what kind of wood it's made from." Unidentifiable wood, no central post, no means of support. None of it made sense.

"Miracles do still happen."

"Really?"

Her eyes widened. "Oh yes. There are many, especially surrounding the saints."

He did remember some interesting stories when his confirmation class studied some of the saints. Their lives just always seemed so far removed from his own. "Yeah, I guess so." *Don't know how else you'd explain it.* He pulled his vibrating phone from his pocket.

Miss you.

Jenna. He sent a quick reply. *Miss you too. We are in Santa Fe right now at this awesome old church.*

He was composing another message, describing the staircase, when her response came through.

Cool. I'm heading to the pool with the girls. Then we're off to the mall. I'll send some pics. Bye!

He deleted the message he was working on. She wouldn't understand his fascination anyway. Instead, he typed two simple words.

Have fun.

He stuffed the phone back in his jeans, frustration suddenly burning through him. Hanging out at the pool with everyone was how he was supposed to spend the summer. But instead, his friends were creating great memories together while he was stuck in the middle of nowhere, pretending to have fun. He glanced back toward the small chapel. Then again, if he were at home, he wouldn't have seen the miraculous staircase.

Grandma handed the clerk a couple dollars to pay for the postcards, then glanced at Luke. "Maybe you can find something for your sweetheart here."

His gaze scanned the store of mostly religious items. "I don't know. Her family doesn't go to church very often. I don't think she'd appreciate anything from here."

Grandma took the bag from the clerk with a smile of thanks. "I told your dad I'd meet him at the park in the plaza. Want to walk over with me?"

"Sure." He held the door open for her, then escorted his grandmother toward the center of the historic downtown. "It was interesting hearing how you and Grandpa met."

"Thank you. It has always been one of my favorite stories, but Charlie never wanted to make known his deviant ways."

He shook his head. "He wasn't a deviant. He was a hero for saving that dog." Besides, hearing about the rebel side of his by-the-book Grandpa somehow made Luke feel closer to him.

"That's exactly what I always told him, but he was never convinced."

As they neared the tourist shops that lined the streets and began to filter through the crowd of tourists, Grandma wrapped her arm around Luke's. "Tell me more about this girl of yours."

What fun—talking girls with Grandma. He plastered on a smile. "What do you want to know?"

"How did you meet?"

He veered her around a family that had suddenly stopped to snap a photo. "We don't have an interesting story like you and Grandpa. We've been in the same group of friends for years. Her best friend and one of my friends started dating, and since their parents didn't want them going on dates alone, they asked us to go with them. We just hit it off, I guess."

"You told me she doesn't go to church and that you don't talk much. But you must have things in common . . . otherwise, you wouldn't like her."

She's not gonna let this go, is she? Grandma may have missed her calling as an investigative reporter with those bloodhound skills of pursuing a story. "Yeah, she's cool. We do things like go to the movies, school sporting events, and group stuff."

"Are you two pretty serious?"

Funny, even though he'd rather be discussing practically anything else right now, the questions weren't quite as annoying coming from Grandma as they would have been if Mom were the one doing the snooping. "Yeah, I guess so."

"What happens when you go off to college?"

That fastball from left field left him speechless. College? He hadn't even started his senior year yet. His parents had made him visit a few campuses, but it all felt too overwhelming.

"You could check out Benedictine College where Harry teaches. It's a wonderful school."

He swallowed the lump in his throat. "Umm . . . I haven't thought much about it. To tell you the truth, I don't like thinking about being separated from Jenna or any of my friends. They're like the most important people to me."

She patted his arm. "I'm glad you have such a good group of friends. You've always been like your grandfather, easily making friends wherever you go. I've never told you this, but how you easily juggle your different acquaintances is quite impressive. Remember that birthday party when you invited all your favorite friends but hardly any of them knew each other? I was amazed how you made them all feel comfortable. It didn't take long before everyone was playing together, like they'd been friends for years."

He shrugged, thinking back to all the different groups he used to hang out with. It was easy back then to merge friend groups. That didn't work so well anymore. In fact, to make life easier, he now, almost exclusively, hung out with his football teammates.

Grandma continued. "It's nice that Jenna is part of your friend group. Having a lot in common with someone you're dating is important so you feel comfortable talking about anything."

Never expected to get relationship advice from my grandmother, but I suppose fifty years of marriage gives her some credibility. He wasn't sure though if her words of wisdom described Jenna. She was fun to hang out with, but they'd never really discussed anything deep.

They rounded a corner and came upon the square-shaped plaza, a centralized park surrounded by streets lined with red adobe stores. They joined the crowd of tourists strolling past the displays of handcrafted items, admiring the wood carvings, paintings, and woven blankets set up along the sidewalks.

His elderly companion stopped to admire a stand of Southwestern jewelry. "I bought a postcard to send to Harry. I have a few extras. Would you like to send one to Jenna?"

The woman was nothing if not persistent. "Maybe." He had no idea what he'd write, though. It would have to be something witty, smooth, and slightly romantic since Jenna would most likely show it to everyone or post it online. If it were sappy, he'd never live it down.

"These pieces of jewelry are pretty. Would she like one of these?"

Luke leaned in for a better look at the turquoise necklaces. While no expert on Jenna's taste in jewelry, he was pretty confident the whole Native American look was not her style. Unless it could be purchased at the mall, she'd have no interest.

"There you two are." Dad squeezed Luke's shoulder. "How about we all shop here for a half-hour or so, then we can grab lunch? The volunteer at the chapel told me which places have the best green chili."

Luke raised an eyebrow. "Are you sure you can handle authentic green chili, old man?" Speaking of being compatible—Dad and spicy foods were not a match made in heaven. While he claimed to enjoy it, the tears that inevitably streamed down his cheeks told a different story.

"I'm willing to give it a shot. Can't come to New Mexico and not try their specialty."

Grandma gave Dad's arm a gentle squeeze. "You take after your father. Charlie couldn't handle spicy foods, either."

Luke nudged his dad with an elbow. "Thank you for not passing that gene on to me."

Grandma lifted her bag of postcards. "While you all shop, I'm going to find a shady spot on one of the benches in the park and write my postcard to Harry. Just come get me before you head to the restaurant."

"Sure thing, Mom." Dad watched her make her way to the center of the square, then turned to Luke. "All right, let's check out these souvenirs."

Luke glanced at his grandma as she settled onto a bench. Maybe she was right and he should send Jenna a postcard. A whole letter would be way too daunting, but a postcard might be a good idea. He watched as Grandma pulled a pen out of her purse and leaned over to write then hurried to catch up with his dad, glad to have a moment alone with him.

"Hey, Dad. As an architect, what did you think of that staircase?"

His dad's forehead creased. "What do you mean?"

Luke shoved a hand into his pocket. "I don't know. I guess, I'm having trouble believing it's really a miracle."

His dad nodded and slowed his pace. "While it is hard to wrap our minds around, there's no denying that scientists and engineers haven't been able to explain it."

Luke hovered behind as his dad leaned over to look at a table full of silver belt buckles. "But if there are miracles happening around us, why don't people know about them? Wouldn't that knowledge turn more people to the Church?"

His dad turned his gaze toward him. "I think people need to be ready to believe. If they don't already have faith, all the proof in the world couldn't convince them." He held up a large belt buckle in the shape of a steer's head. "Hey, we could get matching souvenirs."

Luke grimaced. "Thanks, but no thanks." He turned and looked in the direction of the church. "But I do think I'm going to run back to the chapel and buy a picture of that staircase. I don't ever want to forget it. Then we can go check out that green chili of yours."

Grandma

Harry,

We are now in Santa Fe. It's as beautiful as I remember. So far, we are having a wonderful time, but I haven't found a way to tell them the real reason I wanted to take this trip. Hopefully, the moment will present itself soon.

Your loving sister,
Grace

Chapter 6

Austin:
Away from Keyboard

He sprinted down the hill, moving as fast as his legs could churn. Weapon in hand, he was ready to end this battle. A quick dodge around an overturned barrel and a leap over a fallen tree didn't slow him down. When he landed, he opened fire.

"Austin!" Mom's sing-song call interrupted his game. *Really?* He'd spent the entire day with the family exploring Santa Fe. Couldn't he have just a few minutes alone? Besides, his legs still ached from climbing those sand dunes. Although, he would've been happy staying there a few more days and exploring.

Something hit the side of the tent, then slid down the outside. "Out, dweeb. Put the stupid game away."

Luke's demand greatly decreased Austin's desire to leave the tent.

"Luke!"

Austin pictured the stern, furrow-browed look that almost certainly accompanied Mom's scolding.

Where does he get off giving me a hard time about using my phone? Luke was constantly texting and sending pictures to his stupid girlfriend. Talk about a toxic relationship. They might as well be hazardous waste. And why didn't Luke razz Celia about using her phone? Her earbuds were permanently attached. But of course, she was the favorite child, always getting her way—one way or the other.

As if it weren't torture enough to hang out with his siblings for a month in a motorhome, he also had to sleep next to Luke every night in the tent. He'd begged Celia to join them, hoping the three of them could continue the fun they'd had at the dunes, but apparently, he was the only sibling who wanted that. Celia had refused his request, and Luke had left not a single shadow of doubt that any fun they'd had earlier was a one-off. At least Luke didn't try to scare him with ghost stories or anything. The silent treatment was better than that.

Funny, he'd traded in one miserable camping experience for another. Mom, of course, had signed him up for the usual week of church camp this summer, but since those activities had ceased being fun, he'd been happy that this trip had gotten him out of going. He used to enjoy hanging out with the kids his age at church, but as they'd gotten older, most had become involved in sports or other activities, and youth group had suddenly ranked low on their list of priorities. Now only a few people remained, making it more awkward than fun. If only he could find some activity that interested him, then he'd also have an excuse to stop attending.

He rolled onto his side, ready to get lost in his game again.

"Austin," Grandma's sweet-as-cotton-candy voice called. "You've got to come see this."

He flopped onto his back and huffed out a breath. *Fine. I'll do it. For Grandma.* Because, despite his siblings' half-hearted assurances, he still wondered if she was sick.

Sorry, world, no time to save you from a zombie apocalypse. He exited the game and shoved the phone under his pillow. Poking his head out of the tent, he spotted the campfire. Cool. How had he missed the crackling sounds and smoky smell? Mom patted the empty chair next to her.

"Cool fire," he muttered as he plopped into the chair. Mom had bought a windchime from one of the vendors earlier in the day, and it now hung near the door of the RV. Its melodious tinkle and the popping of the embers were in stark contrast to the chaotic battle sounds of his game.

Grandma sent a warm smile his way. "It's beautiful, isn't it? I knew you wouldn't want to miss it."

When did it get so dark? How long had he been in the tent? Clouds blanketed the night sky, covering the stars, but at least there was no rain in sight tonight.

"Here." Celia tossed him a stick. "Now that you're *finally* here, we can make s'mores."

Austin avoided any eye contact as the s'more items made their way around the campfire circle. Even though his stomach betrayed him—thrilled to be there—the rest of him was not. Siena attentively watched the process in case anyone dropped a tasty treat. When all items made it safely around without an ounce of droppage, she plopped down at Dad's feet.

Austin's mouth was the next body part to succumb to the activity, watering as he balanced the graham cracker and chocolate on his knee. He shoved a marshmallow on the stick and hovered it over the fire.

"So . . ." Luke slid two puffy white marshmallows on his stick. Did he always have to one-up everyone? "Whose turn is it to tell a story tonight?" His gaze flicked toward Austin.

Austin concentrated on the task at hand, slowly turning his stick to warm all sides of the marshmallow. *No way. Not my turn.* As interesting as Grandma's tale was, he had hoped everyone would forget about the storytelling idea. Anything he might mention would just be ridiculed by Luke and Celia. Better to keep quiet.

Dad broke the heavy silence. "I'll go. I've got this one story from high school that's pretty good."

Prepare thyself for unparalleled boredom with some teachable moment. Dad was too much of a by-the-rules kind of guy to have any entertaining stories.

Dad cleared his throat. "So, this one day, a couple of buddies talked me into ditching class."

No way! He stared at Dad, shocked by this admission.

"*You* ditched class?" Celia seemed equally astonished.

Dad had a rebellious side? Granted, growing up with a father who was a judge probably made it nearly impossible to get away with anything.

A crooked grin slid across Dad's face. Austin gawked. He could clearly see the mischievous teenager lurking beneath the familiar respectable-father demeanor. "The plan was to meet by this certain stairwell and then sneak up to the roof to hang out for a while. After my third-period class, I hurried to our meeting place and found Jimmy and Gary waiting for me."

Grandma pulled her stick out of the fire to check on her marshmallow. "Oh, yes. I remember this incident." She rotated her stick and sent it back toward the flames.

"They were pretty good guys. We just had a momentary lapse in judgement." Dad slid his gooey marshmallow between the graham cracker pieces. "Jimmy was a pretty hefty guy, and Gary had recently broken his arm, so it was in a cast. Anyway, I remember being so nervous as we snuck up the stairs as quietly as we could and eased open the heavy door to the roof. I even thought to place a notebook in the doorway so it wouldn't close all the way."

Dad's pause to take a bite of his dessert provided Austin the perfect moment to check the progress of his own marshmallow. A perfect golden brown. His stomach rumbled as he pulled it from the fire.

"How high up were you?" Mom waved away a billow of smoke wafting her way.

"That section of the building was only two stories high. But the view was great. We could see for miles." Dad popped a bite into his mouth. "We were up there about forty minutes or so just chatting, then we decided to head back down. But when we got to the door, it was closed. And locked."

"What happened?" Austin sank his teeth into the delectable sandwich.

"I never did find out if the notebook somehow slipped out, or someone removed it."

Celia licked her fingers. "So, what'd you do?"

As if he could read minds, Dad passed the dessert items around the circle again in case anyone wanted seconds. "Remember, this was before cell phones. We couldn't just call someone to come rescue us. We thought about waiting until somebody passed by and yelling down at them. But of course, unless it happened to be one of our friends, they would have to tell the office, and we'd be in huge trouble. We sure didn't want anyone calling our folks." He winked at Grandma.

"And I thought you were such a good boy," she teased.

Austin slipped his next marshmallow onto his stick. "What happened next?" Dad was as bad as Grandma at getting to the exciting part of the story.

Dad leaned back in his chair, stretching his legs out in front of him. "We did what any young male would do—looked for a way off the roof. And we found one. There was a metal fire escape ladder. But it didn't go all the way to the ground. It stopped halfway down. The good news was, it was now our lunch period, so we weren't missing anything important. But we didn't see it that way. We were teenage boys and starving. We needed to get off that stupid roof and to the cafeteria. Since I was the most mobile of the group, I climbed onto the fire escape and tried to figure out how to lower the ladder the rest of the way. It's a good thing there wasn't a fire, because I could not for the life of me figure out how it worked."

Engrossed in the story, Austin neglected his second marshmallow, which suddenly burst into flames. "Ahh!"

"Smooth."

Luke's sarcasm was even more infuriating than the ruined snack. Austin felt like flicking the charred mess at his brother, but then karma struck, igniting Luke's marshmallow, as well. The shock of silence was soon followed by laughter—from everyone.

Luke grinned at Austin. "Can someone answer my *burning* question?"

"Can we have *s'more?*" Austin joked back, his annoyance sizzling away like the puffy mallows.

The stupid puns made everyone laugh even harder. Each time they began to control themselves, someone started up again with a giggle, or a snort, and the contagious merriment spread again. Soon, they were all suffering from sore sides and streaming tears.

Best moment of the day.

Once they'd all finally settled, Dad wiped his eyes and continued his tale. "Okay, back to the story. From where I was on the fire escape, it was still too high to jump down. But there was a window ledge and an open window not far from me. My heart pounded like crazy, but I climbed onto the handrail, then somehow maneuvered my feet to the window. I pushed myself away from the fire escape and slid through the window. My back scraped against the bricks, but I didn't care about the pain. I was so thankful to be inside. That's when I glanced around. There were three sinks and three stalls, one of which was occupied. Then it hit me. There were no urinals." He paused a beat. "I was in a girls' bathroom."

Mom leaned forward. "This is getting interesting."

The flickering light from the fire made it hard to be sure, but Dad's cheeks looked a little red. "I needed to get out of there—fast. But I wanted to do it quietly, so I slowly opened the door, backed out, and let the door silently shut. I was so relieved to be out of that bathroom and let out a huge sigh. All I could think about was that I needed to rescue my friends. If I hurried, we could still grab something to eat before our next class. Ready to scurry up the stairs to the roof door, I turned around." He stopped and glanced around the fire, looking at each person.

"Yeah, then what?" Celia prompted, her eyes wide.

Dad rubbed his hand over his mouth before talking. "A roomful of teachers stared at me as I snuck out of the women's bathroom into the teachers' lounge."

Classic!

Luke threw his head back and laughs. "No way!"

"What did they say?" Celia's eyes grew even round-er.

Dad shook his head. "I don't remember exactly, but I do recall having to spend the rest of the day in the principal's office, trying to explain."

Grandma pulled her sweater tighter around her. "Which was probably far easier than when you had to explain it to your father that night at dinner."

Dad let out a little snort, giving him that naugh-ty-teen look again. "You got that right. I think I was grounded for a week. But I guess it was worth the pun-ishment since it makes for a great story now."

Another awesome tale. Maybe it wasn't such a dumb idea after all.

The laughter and comments slowly died down to match the smoldering fire. Everyone was lost in their own thoughts as they watched the burning logs crum-ble, sending sparks shooting into the air.

"Oh my." Grandma pointed to the sky.

During Dad's story, the clouds had parted to reveal millions of twinkling stars. *Whoa.* "Why are there so many tonight?" Austin breathed.

"They're always there, sweetie." Mom squeezed his hand. "We usually can't see so many of them because of all the city lights."

"Really?" He leaned back, mesmerized by the view. How did he not know there were so many visible stars in the sky? He really needed to get out of the house more often.

Chapter 7

Celia:
A Dull Silver Lining

The hovering shadow forced Celia to slam her notebook shut. Ready to lash out at her brothers for interrupting, her eyes instead focused on Grandma's smiling face.

"Mind if I join you?"

Celia had been enjoying the alone time but certainly was not going to say that to her grandmother. "Of course not." She scooched to the edge of the bench to give Grandma plenty of room.

"It's pretty here, isn't it?" Grandma sighed as she settled in.

Pretty might be an apt word for a field of wildflowers, but it didn't really fit the valley of pale, rolling hills before them. Although, no appropriate adjective came to mind to describe the subtle stripes of blues and greens that gave the landscape an alien-world vibe. "Yeah, I've never seen anything like this before." While the boys were fascinated with the fossilized wood scattered throughout today's stop, the Petrified Forest National Park, Celia preferred the scene in front of her—the enchanting Blue Mesa Trail—especially since the rest of the family opted to hike around the unique landscape, allowing her some alone time.

Grandma looked down at the notebook on Celia's lap. "Were you journaling or something? I didn't mean to disturb you."

Celia resisted the urge to make something up, since Grandma seemed a trustworthy confidant. "No, I was sketching."

Grandma's thin eyebrows rose. "May I see?"

"Um . . ." Celia had never shown anyone her drawings before, always afraid of what people would say. Luckily, Grandma lacked Luke's arsenal of biting comments. "Okay." She flipped open to the page she'd been working on.

Grandma sucked in a breath. "Oh, Celia." She reached out, her wrinkled hand barely touching the page. "This is wonderful. How did I not know you were so talented?"

Celia couldn't help the smile that snuck onto her face, even if the compliment came from someone who loved her unconditionally and probably wasn't a reliable critic. "Thanks. I don't really show people my work."

Grandma leaned closer to the drawing. "You get your talent from your father and great-grandmother. The gift certainly skipped my generation. Neither Harry nor I could draw a stick figure."

"Dad?" Even though he was an architect and designed buildings, she'd never thought of him as particularly artistic. He was more of a computer geek.

"Oh, sure." Grandma straightened to look at her. "He used to always be drawing one thing or the other."

"Really?" She and Dad actually had something in common? She resumed her work of shading the mounds she'd just penciled in.

"I wish I could have sketched like that when we traveled. I tried a few times, but it only became clear I did not inherit my mother's gift. It must have become clear to her, as well, since that's about the time she bought my first diary." The creases around Grandma's eyes deepened as she laughed.

It was good to see Grandma so happy. "So, what did you write about?"

Grandma's eyes lit up. "At first, I just wrote about where we went and what we saw, as well as a few childhood musings. Over time, I started reflecting a little more on life issues."

"Philosophical stuff? Like the mystery of life?"

"I don't know if I was that deep." Grandma chuckled. "But at some point, my diary transformed into a prayer journal."

Celia glanced up. "A prayer journal?"

"Oh, yes. If you've never tried it, I'd highly recommend starting one. It's fascinating to look back and see how your prayers have been answered."

A heavy sigh snuck out before Celia could stop it. She didn't need a journal to keep track of the answers to her prayers. All year she'd been praying and either God wasn't listening or was stubbornly sticking to His answer of no.

Grandma, of course, didn't miss the reaction. "The reason I enjoy looking back through my prayer requests, is when you're in the midst of something, it's very hard to see, but He does answer all our prayers."

Celia focused on her sketch, willing the conversation to end.

But Grandma didn't let it drop. "You know, Harry once told me something that has stayed with me. He said, 'God has two responses to our prayers. *Yes.* And *no, because.*' While it makes no sense to us when our prayers aren't answered, God sees a larger plan for our lives. So, His no could mean several things. No, because that would not be good for you. No, because you aren't ready yet. Or no, because I have a better plan for you."

Celia turned to look at Grandma. While she didn't want to admit it out loud, the theory was worth contemplating.

Grandma reached over and squeezed Celia's hand. "For instance, I prayed a lot that Walter Murphy would notice me. But God knew that was not the man for me. So, His answer was 'No, because you have not yet met the man who will become your husband.'" Grandma's gaze turned toward the beautiful landscape. "Looking back on my prayer journal makes it clear how God has been guiding my life."

Celia stared out at the rolling canyon in front of them. While she had dreaded this month of family togetherness, the thought of going back to the status quo completely threatened her contented mood. Life back at home was miserable. For months, she'd focused her prayers on life going back to the way it had been. When those prayers weren't answered, she'd given up. *Could God's silence really be steering me in a new direction?* Celia tucked the thought away for another day's pondering.

"That's cool that you and Harry could talk about such deep things. You're lucky." If she had a sibling she could confide in, maybe re-evaluating her life wouldn't be necessary.

Grandma's eyes narrowed, like she was reading Celia's thoughts. "Harry and I were close, but that doesn't mean we didn't argue and have moments when we didn't get along. All siblings have those times. Especially when you have brothers." She shared a conspiratorial wink. "We both know how annoying boys can be."

A little laugh escaped at that unexpected comment. Celia smiled. "You got that right."

- - - X - - -

The surest way to stall a conversation was to serve dinner, especially when campfire burgers were on the menu. Just as Celia sank her teeth into her meal, Austin slammed his fist down on the picnic table. Everyone jumped at the sudden bang. All eyes focused on him.

"Story time," he proclaimed.

Luke shoved Austin's shoulder. "Dude! Trying to give someone a heart attack?"

Grandma clapped her hands together. "Sounds like a wonderful idea. Whose turn is it?"

Thanks a lot, twerp. Celia finished chewing the hunk of meat in her mouth. Amazing how two words could make a savory meal lose its flavor. So much for letting everyone forget this idea. *Hopefully, they won't force someone to participate.* She didn't have a single thing she wished to share.

"I'll go." Mom broke the heavy silence. "I was once in a movie." She ended her statement by popping a chunk of potato in her mouth.

Celia stared at her mother in stunned silence, the words circling around her brain. *Did she just say she was in a movie?* She glanced at Luke, who sat frozen, his burger positioned in front of his open mouth. He met her gaze with an equally mystified look. Austin's mouth also gaped open. Thank goodness he hadn't started eating yet.

"Mom." Celia winced at the whine in her voice. "You can't just drop a bombshell like that and not explain."

Mom grinned, then pushed her plate away. "Okay. It was the summer after my freshman year of high school, and I had gone with my friend Emily and her family to San Diego for a week. We were staying at her uncle's beach house and had big plans to lounge by the ocean all week and work on our tans. The first day we were there, we noticed a lot of commotion down the beach, so we wandered over. That's when we found out that a few scenes for a movie were being filmed there. How cool was that? We hung around, watching. Then one of the crew members came over and asked if we'd like to be extras in the film. Well, of course, we said yes! So, we spent three days running around the beach in the background of the scenes that were being filmed." She gave them a funny smile, then took a sip of her iced tea.

Unbelievable.

"No way!" Austin's hand pounded the table, rattling the plates again. "That's so cool!"

"Why didn't you ever tell us?" Seemed like something to brag about.

Mom shot a quick glance toward Dad as she set down her glass. "Well, I told your father about it, but there never was a good time to mention it to you kids."

"What movie?" Luke finally lowered his uneaten burger. "Is it something we've seen?"

Mom shook her head. "I sure hope not." She lowered her gaze and smoothed invisible wrinkles out of the plastic tablecloth. "It was actually a dumb teen slasher movie." When she looked up again, a noticeable blush colored her cheeks. "I wasn't even allowed to watch it when it first came out. It was about the ghost of an old sea captain who was upset about a planned amusement park being built at the beach. He was determined to stop the project by killing everyone."

"That sounds stupid." Austin summed up Celia's thoughts before taking a giant bite of his burger.

Mom let out a little laugh. "Oh, it was. I never told you because it's not something that I'd ever let you watch. But maybe, when we get back home, I can show you the scene I was in. The video is so grainy, but if you look very closely, you can see Emily and me in the background."

Mom in a movie. Never would have guessed that in a million years. Who knew this dumb idea of Grandma's would be so revealing?

Grandma

Dear Diary,

That seems so corny to write. Since I've never had a diary before, I have no idea what I'm doing, but that seems like the logical way to start. But honestly, I don't get it. Who exactly am I writing to? You? You're a notebook. Why am I telling you about my day? Myself? Doesn't really make sense since I just lived it. God? He already knows everything. Hopefully, not Harry or Mom or Dad—that would be so embarrassing.

This particular journal didn't come with any diary-keeping instructions. But I need to use it since Mom bought it for me just for the trip. When I opened the package, she explained that every young lady needs a place to write her thoughts and feelings. I had no idea I was missing out.

Anyway, we are on our way. Our great summer adventure to the Southwest has begun. I don't know what to expect. I keep picturing cowboys and Indians galloping their horses across the desert. Harry laughed when I told him this and said I'd watched too many Lone Ranger episodes—which is his fault since I don't even like that show—except for Silver the horse—he's so pretty. I guess I'll see for myself what New Mexico and Arizona look like soon enough. We're loaded into the sedan, the silver camper trailing behind us. I've got a stack of Nancy Drew books to keep me entertained.

And now I also have this nifty new diary. Time for this summer vacation to begin.

Gracie (Obviously, who else would be writing in my diary?)

Chapter 8

LUKE:
FOUL BALL

Luke stared at the incredible crucifix hanging above the altar. It was like nothing he'd ever seen before. Christ nailed to a tree. A tree. Not a cross, but a tree. The branches even had leaves hanging on them. Between that and the view behind the cross—the stunning red rocks of Sedona—it had been a little hard to keep his head in the game as the family had taken time to pray in front of the unusual crucifix. Grandma had told them this church was special. She hadn't been wrong. She continually proved to be a woman of her word.

His gaze flicked over to her as she knelt in prayer, rosary beads in hand. Next to him, Celia sat back and made the sign of the cross. He did a double take as her fingers brushed her cheek. *Was that a tear she wiped away or just a strand of hair?* When she stood to leave, Luke followed her out the church doors, hoping for a chance to chat.

"This place is so beautiful." She stood in the middle of the patio, staring at the massive red rocks shooting into the air around them.

Quite the understatement. The church, Chapel of the Holy Cross, was built into the rocks, becoming part of the landscape. Questions swirled. Who would think to build a church here? How did they construct it?

"This has got to be my favorite church ever." Austin joined them, bringing along the scent of the incense that had wafted through the sanctuary.

Luke pushed his ponderings aside and glanced back to make sure they were alone. "Hey, do you think Grandma seems different today?"

Celia peeled her gaze away from the scenery to look at him, shielding her eyes from the sun. "What do you mean?"

"I don't know. She just seems a little out of it. Not her usual happy self." Luke wasn't exactly sure what felt off, but something didn't seem right.

Celia bit her lower lip. "Maybe she's just tired. That was quite a walk up here; it could have worn her out."

Luke surveyed the route to the entrance. A few reps of running up and down that steep, winding path would be a killer leg workout. "Yeah . . . maybe."

Austin shook his head. "I don't think that's it. She was quiet at breakfast, too. Do you think she really is sick?" His gaze bored into Luke—like just because he's older, he should have all the answers.

Don't I wish. "Maybe." If that was the case, then he was thankful they'd agreed to this trip. If something were to happen to her and they had refused to come, he never would have forgiven himself.

The adults made their way out of the chapel, Grandma's thin arm wrapped around Dad's.

"So, what did you all think of the chapel?" Mom asked.

"It's stunning and perfectly highlights the beauty of the area. Something about it made me want to pray." The words gushed out of Celia's mouth. This from the girl who'd lately huffed in protest when kneeling at Mass. Good. Maybe she'd finally come to terms with whatever demons had been haunting her all year.

Grandma nodded. "They did a beautiful job of not only drawing your focus to Christ with that amazing cross, but the building's design really emphasizes God's glorious creation."

"I bet it was cool to see again," Austin said.

Grandma slowly shook her head. "It was under construction when we were here last." Her eyes scanned the area. "My parents would have loved to have experienced this."

That must be what's bothering Grandma today—she's missing her family. Mystery solved, Luke shifted his attention to his father. "Hey, Dad, how on earth do they build something like this?"

Dad chuckled. "It usually starts with some crazy architect who comes up with a beautiful but illogical design, and then the engineers somehow find a way to make it work."

Luke looked back at the chapel. How cool it would be to be part of something so amazing.

Dad's hand rested on Luke's shoulder. "If you think this is spectacular, wait until you see the skywalk at the Grand Canyon. Ever since it was built, along the western rim, I've wanted to check it out. It's truly an engineering marvel."

"There's a new structure along the west rim?" Grandma sounded surprised.

Dad nodded. "Yeah, a few years ago, they built a huge visitor center and a walkway that juts out into the canyon."

"Cool!" Austin exclaimed.

Mom shivered. "Sounds terrifying."

Dad clapped his hands together. "But that's a few days away. Today we explore Sedona. Anyone feel like hiking?"

Celia and Luke both silently nodded their affirmation.

"Absolutely!" Austin's enthusiastic answer received some disapproving glances from the exiting tourists. Mom and Dad didn't even seem to notice.

Must be nice being the favorite child. If he or Celia had ever done that, they would've been reprimanded, or at least gotten the ole evil eye.

"Not me." Mom reached into her purse and pulled out her sunglasses. "I'm planning an afternoon of browsing through the shops in town. Anyone need anything?"

Celia lifted her hair off her neck. "Would you buy me a few summery tops or T-shirts? It's really hot here."

Gee, what a surprise. Wearing black in the middle of the summer, in the desert, was hot.

Mom unfolded one of the brochures she'd picked up in the church and fanned Celia. "Sure thing. Grace, do you want to join me?"

Grandma took a deep breath. "Yes, that would be lovely. If I get tired, I can always find a nice little café to sit and read." She patted her bag that probably contained her Bible and her leather diary she'd been toting around. "I may also try to call Harry."

Mom smiled at her mother-in-law. "Good. Sounds like we have a plan for the day."

Luke glanced at Celia. That definitely was not like Grandma. She enjoyed exploring, not sitting around. His initial instincts were spot on. Something was not right. He focused on Grandma. Did she look more tired than usual? Worn out? Sick? Worried? He had no trouble reading a quarterback's expressions, knowing exactly what the passer was thinking on the field, but Grandma? She remained a mystery.

Dad pointed back to the church. "Mom, there's an elevator down to the street level. Do you want to take that?"

Grandma set her jaw in determination. "No. It's too beautiful here to not enjoy every moment. Let's just walk slowly."

There. *That's more like the grandma we all know and love.*

- - - X - - -

Luke collapsed into one of the folding chairs at their campsite. If his burning leg muscles could rejoice, they would. The hike had been incredible, but exhausting. He was in much better shape than Dad or his siblings. They really had to be hurting. A glance in their direction confirmed it—at least partially. Dad and Austin were both slumped in their chairs, heads tilted back, eyes shut. Even Siena, sprawled next to Austin, was worn out—no easy task. Celia, on the other hand, was hunched over her notebook working away at something.

As he shifted to a more comfortable position, the phone in his back pocket jabbed his hip, which made him think back to the hike. They had climbed to a rock ledge that overlooked this incredible red rock canyon. The photos he'd taken of the colorful cliffs against the deep blue sky perfectly captured the amazing view. Until that moment, he'd never understood how people felt so connected with nature. Being up there with just his thoughts had been awesome. Why did it take getting out of town to realize this? It had been such a perfect moment that he'd wanted to share it with someone. Sure, he'd technically experienced it with his family, but he'd had this urge to share it with Jenna.

Her response, though, was not what he'd expected. Not sure how he'd wanted her to respond, but not, "Cool. Hey, you'll never guess what I did last night." Total buzzkill. Her complete lack of interest had ruined the moment. To be fair, it wasn't her fault—none of his friends would get it, because it was impossible to explain how, or why, all these sites affected him. It just had to be experienced to be understood.

After five more incoming messages about her "amazing" night, he'd turned his phone off and stuffed it in his pocket. He'd just wanted to enjoy every moment of the hike and the incredible scenery without distractions. *She's probably freaking out right about now.* He leaned his head back and closed his eyes, forgetting the drama and instead, picturing the scenic wonders from today.

"Hey, what do you think?"

He lifted his head, surprised to see Celia watching him. "You talking to me?"

She let out a little laugh. "Of course. Those two are dead to the world." She angled her notebook toward him.

No way. He sat up. "Wow. You drew that?"

She smirked at his obvious disbelief. He'd always figured her notebook scribblings were haunting music lyrics or moody poems or something. *Has she always had this much talent?* The picture before him was an exact replica of the canyon they'd just hiked.

"That's amazing."

She squinted her eyes. "Are you being serious?"

He held up a hand. "Scout's honor."

"You weren't a scout."

He put as much sincerity in his voice as possible. "I'm serious; it's great."

"Well . . . thanks." A funny little smile graced her face. Almost more surprising than the fact she could draw was that she seemed to want his approval.

He glanced at her lap, assuming that her drawing was a copy from a photo, but she only held her notebook and a few colored pencils. "Did you draw that from memory?"

She turned the notebook around to look at the drawing. "Yeah."

He grabbed his phone and turned it on. "Your drawing is an exact match to my photos." Ignoring the now twelve texts from Jenna, he pulled up his photos. "Look." He walked over to Celia's chair.

As they were comparing the two images, his phone buzzed—again.

Celia shot him a slant-eyed glance. "Apparently, someone misses you."

"Yeah." His shoulders sagged at the thought of reading Jenna's monotonous updates of her day. It wasn't that he minded hearing what she'd been up to, but it was frustrating that she never cared what he'd been doing. Like his updates were somehow in the way of her posts.

Celia tucked a strand of hair behind her ear. "You don't miss her?"

He plopped back down in his chair, his muscles thanking him. "No, it's not that. I do miss her. It's just, all she wants to talk about is what's happening back home. She has no interest at all in what I've been doing."

Celia tapped the pencil she was holding against her chin. "Maybe she doesn't want you to feel like you're missing out on everything."

Wow. Wonders never ceased. Celia hadn't swung at the low-hanging ball he'd given her to trash Jenna. "Well, if that's her plan, I guess it's working, because I can't tell you how thankful I am not to have to live the monotony. Reading about it is painful enough."

Celia let out another chuckle. Two laughs in one conversation? She was on a roll.

"Seriously," he continued, glad to have someone to talk to about what had been bothering him. "How much can there be to say about malls, shopping, and movie nights?"

"Hearing her updates doesn't make you wish you were back home?"

"Not really." *Huh. Interesting.* "I thought it would be the worst thing to be away, but somehow, I don't care that much." Even though his friends were all doing stuff without him, for some reason, it didn't really bug him.

She glanced toward Dad, still conked out, then leaned back in her chair. "Yeah, this trip isn't as horrible as I thought it would be."

He couldn't have said it better himself.

Celia closed her sketch pad and began putting her colored pencils away. She held an orange-y one in front of her. "I've been using this color a lot lately. It's burnt sienna. Do you remember how we decided on Siena's name?"

He stared at the pencil as memories flooded back. "Oh yeah. We kept arguing about what to name her. Her puppy coat was a lot darker, and you insisted we call her Cinnamon."

She pushed the pencil in the case with the others. "Austin wanted to name her something dumb, like Peaches. Thank goodness Mom's friend thought her fur looked like the color sienna."

He chuckled. "I totally forgot about that. Didn't you insist we call the poor lady Siena's fairy dog-mother?"

She stifled a laugh, then leaned forward and pointed a finger at him. "But you didn't want a dog named after a color, so we had to change the spelling."

He threw his hands out in front of him. "Well, yeah. That was almost as bad as Peaches. But then at confirmation class, they were discussing Saint Catherine of Siena, so I graciously conceded to the name if it was spelled like the city."

"So chivalrous of you." She grinned and shook her head. "Hey, since Mom and Grandma aren't back yet and Dad is out like a light, want to help me make dinner?"

His stomach growled at the mere mention of food. "What did you have in mind?"

"I don't know but I'm getting a little tired of hotdogs and hamburgers."

"Yeah, the food repertoire has been a little repetitive. What about personal pizzas? We used to cook them on the grill at home. I bet we could do them over the fire."

She clapped her hands, causing one of Siena's eyes to pop open. "Everyone can make their own! It'll be fun."

"Maybe it'll even cheer up Grandma. We just need to make some dough."

"Let's do it!" She popped out of the chair.

How could her legs not feel like rubber? Did she have a hidden stash of Red Bull?

Without answering any messages, he stuffed his phone in his pocket again and followed his sister into the motorhome.

Chapter 9

Austin:
Damage Per Second

Maybe it was the sound of the tires crunching on the dirt road . . . or the headlights shining on the tent. Whatever the cause, Austin slowly emerged from a deep sleep. The slam of a car door provided the final abrupt end to his restful slumber. Some people were masters of rudeness. He rolled over. *Hey, jerk, ever think that everyone else in the campground is asleep?*

He burrowed further down in the warm sleeping bag, determined to ignore the voices. Time to get back to his dream. He had been on the verge of breaching the outer wall of the castle to battle a horde of beasts.

Knock. Knock.

He jumped, suddenly fully awake. *Is someone knocking on the motorhome door?* Siena confirmed with a low growl.

He glanced at Luke, who rubbed his eyes, then pushed himself up to reach for the zipper of the tent. Their heads together, they peeked out. All was quiet except for the chirping of crickets—most likely expressing their annoyance at being woken in the middle of the night as well. As his eyes adjusted, Austin made out a dark figure at the motorhome door.

What was going on?

The figure reached out an arm. *Knock. Knock.*

Under no circumstances was a visit by a mysterious stranger in the middle of the night good.

From their vantage point, they saw a light flip on inside the motorhome. Then the door opened, revealing Dad, his hair sticking up in odd directions. Mom, wrapped in a robe, and Celia, dressed in a T-shirt and a pair of shorts, appeared behind him.

"Yes?" Dad's gruff voice mumbled. He cleared his throat. "Is something wrong?"

The light from inside the camper illuminated the midnight visitor. A park ranger. *What could he want?*

The ranger removed his hat. "Sorry to disturb you, sir. But I believe I have your mother in my truck."

Austin's head snapped toward Luke. His brother's confused look probably mirrored his own. X-ray vision would be handy so he could peer through the RV to see if Grandma was in her bed where she was supposed to be. Mom and Dad looked at Celia, who disappeared from view for a moment. When she returned, the shake of her head made it clear. Grandma's bed was empty.

The park ranger led Dad out to his truck. Mom and Celia followed along. Luke unzipped the tent the rest of the way and joined the group. Not about to be left behind, Austin kicked his way out of the sleeping bag he was still encased in and scurried out of the tent. His legs protested, still achy from the day's earlier hike. Siena rushed out behind him, barking at the stranger in their midst.

"Shhh." Celia bent down to quiet the noisy canine.

This middle-of-the-night mayhem was probably not the best way to create campground friends. When the park ranger opened the passenger door of his truck, the overhead light created a spotlight on Grandma sitting in the passenger seat.

Her large, shiny eyes scanned the inquiring ones watching her. *Is she about to cry?* Austin swallowed the lump welling up in his throat. He'd never seen Grandma cry. *No way I'm man enough to handle that.* Just as he was about to crawl back into the tent to avoid an overt display of emotion, Grandma let out a loud huff, then stepped out of the vehicle.

"Is it a crime for a person to take a walk?" Her scowl rivaled any Celia had ever delivered—and there had been some doozies. Grandma pushed past Dad and disappeared into the motorhome.

Everyone watched her in stunned silence. When the door slammed shut behind her, Dad turned to the park ranger. "I'm confused. Did you find her out walking by herself?"

The park ranger pointed down the road. "Yeah, a little way down the road."

Dad shared a look with Mom before asking his next question. "Did she say where she was going?"

The ranger scratched his forehead. "No, sir. She wouldn't answer any question except where she was staying."

Dad's jawline clenched, but he extended his arm to shake the ranger's hand. "All right. Thank you for bringing her back safely."

They watched the ranger climb into his truck and back out of the campsite. *Well, now what?*

Mom turned her bleary eyes to the kids. "Celia, do you mind staying out here for a bit while we go talk to her?"

Celia's face transformed from bewilderment to rage. "Seriously? You want me to stand out here, in the dark, in the middle of the night?"

Funny, Austin never realized how much Celia looked like Grandma until tonight with their matching ill-tempered expressions.

Luke reached for their sister's arm as if he was ready to hold her back from storming the RV. "Celia can stay with us the rest of the night."

"Yeah, we have her sleeping bag in there already." Every night since they'd begun this journey, Austin had asked her to join them in the tent, and every night, she'd refused. So, her sleeping bag remained rolled up in the corner of the tent. Looked like being prepared for his hopeful plan had finally come in handy.

"Fine." Celia rolled her eyes and stomped toward the tent.

Luke crawled in after her and flicked on a little battery-operated lantern to give them some light.

Celia plopped down on Austin's sleeping bag. She pulled Siena against her, completely ignoring her red bag wedged in the corner of the tent.

It looked like if there was any chance of sleeping in his own bag, Austin would have to set hers up for her. *Can't she do anything for herself? She-of-perfect-grades can't make her own bed?* With a huff, he grabbed her sleeping bag, drawing a complete blank as to exactly why he'd wanted her to stay with them.

"I can't believe I have to sleep on the ground," she grumbled.

"It's not so bad. It's kind of fun." Austin unrolled her bag with one quick shove. *Not exactly rocket science.*

She shot him a look. "Yeah, real fun."

Luke stretched out on top of his bed. "Why would Grandma wander off in the middle of the night?"

Austin shoved Celia's sleeping bag against the side of the tent. "Maybe she's got that old-person memory thing."

Celia still didn't move, so he attempted to slide into his sleeping bag around her, which finally did the trick.

"Alzheimer's?" She unzipped her bag and slithered in.

"Yeah, that," Austin confirmed.

Luke turned off the light. "I don't know. But going off on her own in the middle of the night is not normal."

"She was really off all day." Celia patted her sleeping bag, and Siena nestled in between her and Austin.

"I know," Luke agreed. "She barely said anything during dinner or when we were playing cards."

"Maybe she'll tell Dad what's wrong." Austin's eyes adjusted to the dark, and he could see Celia's long brown hair trailing out of the red sleeping bag.

Even if his sister was a pain, Austin was glad she was with them. He grinned. The three of them used to do a lot together. But lately, his siblings had had no time for him. He'd never admit it to them, but he secretly hoped this trip might present a chance to hang out together again. Up until now, they hadn't seemed overly interested. Then reality hit, wiping away his smile. The only reason they were all in the tent together was because something was wrong with Grandma. His eyes squeezed shut.

Please, God, help Grandma. Help her to enjoy this trip and stay healthy. And if there's anything we can do to make her happy, please let us know somehow. Amen.

Grandma

Dear Diary,

It's me again. I actually have something to report today. We are at this beautiful campground in Sedona, Arizona. And Harry was right—no cowboys or Indians in sight. But there are pirates! Okay, not really. Just Harry and I pretending to be pirates, but it felt more dramatic to write it that way.

This afternoon, while Mama was lost to her newest painting, Daddy had a meeting at our campsite with someone about local artifacts. As usual, Harry and I were left to our imaginations. That's when we became pirates searching for buried treasure. It was a really fun game.

I'm not sure where Daddy disappeared to, but at one point, we realized that Daddy's friend was watching us. We were embarrassed and stopped what we were doing. But then he explained that he had children of his own. He waved us over and told us he had an idea to make our game even more exciting.

Oh darn. Mama says we have to turn off the lantern and get to sleep. The rest of the tale will have to wait until tomorrow.

Gracie out. (I'm not sure how to sign off on these entries. Nothing quite seems right.)

Chapter 10

Celia:
Out of the Blue

The melodious tweeting of the birds pulled Celia awake. Still exhausted, she attempted to ignore nature's wake-up call. But when she rolled over, something jabbed her hip. *Ow! What is that?* The mattress was usually so comfortable. Her eyes squinted open. Shiny green material came into focus inches from her face. The tent. *Ugh.* How could she forget the impromptu slumber party with the boys? She flipped around to look at her brothers, her back protesting the hard ground.

The sleeping bag on the far side of the tent was empty. Luke must've already gotten up. A quick glance around confirmed that Siena had joined him. Celia sighed. Geez, she must have been exhausted. How'd she sleep through them leaving?

But she wasn't alone. Austin's mop of messy hair stuck out from the top of his sleeping bag. Memories of the three of them sleeping out in their backyard flashed through her mind. One summer, they'd been really into backyard camping. Austin had been pretty little and hadn't always lasted the whole night with Luke and her, but once in a while he had and had been so proud to be hanging out with his older siblings. He'd been kinda cute back then.

How'd things go from that to us barely talking? Tears stung her eyes. Her life was such a mess. She had no friends, her brothers were like strangers, and something was definitely not right with Grandma. Grandma's advice about turning to God with her problems popped into her mind. She'd given it a try at the chapel yesterday, sharing all her anger and frustration through prayer, and had to admit that it left her feeling pretty good.

For months, her pleas to God had remained unanswered. His silence had felt like He'd turned His back on her, so she'd given up. But maybe Grandma had been right, and He had a different plan in mind.

Dear Lord, I'm not even sure what to pray for, but I've been sad for so long. Please help me to somehow turn things around. I'm tired of this lonely life. Can You please lead me out of this dark hole? Thank You. Amen.

She gave it a moment, but no ideas immediately came to mind. *Maybe these things take time.* Ready to face the day, she inched out of the sleeping bag, trying to be quiet so Austin could sleep in. But no matter how slowly she moved, the rustling of the slick material seemed ridiculously loud. She gave up on her attempt to slither out and instead chose the conventional exit and yanked down the zipper. Austin's head popped out of his bag.

"Hey." His face contorted with a yawn as he stretched.

"Morning." She managed to free herself from the bag.

Austin followed her out of the tent where they were greeted by a tail-wagging Siena scurrying over to greet them.

"You been up awhile?" she asked Luke who was slouched down in a chair, ankles crossed.

He rubbed the back of his neck. "Yeah. I couldn't sleep. Guess I had a lot on my mind."

Know what ya mean, big brother. She'd had trouble falling asleep, too, worrying about Grandma and her mysterious midnight excursion. *What was up with her?*

Celia and Austin plopped into chairs, flanking their older brother.

"Where are Mom and Dad?" Austin glanced at the camper.

Luke tilted his head to the left. "They went on a walk."

Celia leaned forward so both boys could hear her whisper. "Have you seen Grandma this morning?"

Luke rolled his head back and forth along the back of the folding chair. "Nope."

Just then, the door of the motorhome opened, and Grandma's head poked out. "Oh, good, you're up." The door flung wide to reveal the tray of food and drinks in her hands. Austin jumped out of his seat and rushed over to help.

The two of them placed the tray of bagels, cream cheese, and orange juice on the picnic table. "Help yourself." Grandma took a coffee mug from the tray and settled into one of the chairs. She appeared perfectly content, as if she hadn't a care in the world, like nothing unusual had happened last night.

Celia glanced at Luke. *Does Grandma even remember last night? Should we bring it up, or ignore it?*

Luke met her gaze. His shoulders hunched up in a small shrug. He then pushed himself out of the chair to head to the table. "Thanks for breakfast, Grandma."

They prepared bagels in silence, then settled back into their chairs. Celia was dying to talk, but didn't know what to say. So instead, she nibbled on her bagel wondering if anyone else was feeling as uncomfortable as she was.

"Story time." Grandma's pronouncement broke the silence.

The three siblings froze in mid-action. Story time? Now? Without Mom and Dad? Grandma really was losing it.

"Umm . . . okay." Luke lowered his orange juice.

Celia finished chewing and waited for the new story to be revealed.

Grandma took a sip of her coffee before beginning. "I told you that each summer, my parents took my brother and me on a road trip to a national park."

Three heads nodded in unison like marionettes controlled by invisible strings.

"And this trip is similar to your favorite one, right?" Celia slowly asked, wary of the response.

Grandma smiled, her eyes focused on her mug. "Right. Traveling with my parents was not like what you're used to with your folks. Your parents like to hike and do fun activities with you. My parents viewed our summers as work trips, not vacation. My father spent most of his time studying or collecting samples. He would often be gone for hours, out interviewing the park rangers or local residents. My mother wiled away the hours sketching and painting."

Celia's mind drifted to her own drawings.

Grandma took another sip of coffee before continuing. "That left Harry and me with a lot of free time to fill. We had active imaginations and created elaborate games to occupy our days. That year, we enjoyed pretending to be pirates searching for buried treasure." She glanced off to the left and grinned, probably remembering their game.

Siena wandered over and laid her head on Grandma's lap. Their family dog had always possessed an uncanny ability to recognize when something wasn't quite right. A wet lick to her hand brought Grandma back to the present. "We were in this very campground, just a few spots over, I think." She stroked the goldendoodle's head.

Celia looked in the direction that her grandmother pointed, trying to picture a younger Grandma and her brother running through the campsite, using sticks as swords.

"One day, our mother was busy painting, and our father was meeting a colleague at our campsite, leaving Harry and I to occupy ourselves. Our father and the gentleman were set up at our picnic table. While they were looking over some artifacts, Harry and I scrambled through the trees playing our pirate game. At one point, our father must have gone into the camper to retrieve some papers or something. Suddenly, we became aware that the man was watching us. We immediately stopped playing, but he smiled and asked what we were doing. We explained we were pirates searching for a long-lost treasure. His eyes lit up, and he told us we weren't the only pirates he had recently met, and that the other ones had dropped off a bag of treasure for him to watch over." She let out a little chuckle. "Harry and I just looked at each other. We weren't used to having adults play-acting with us, so we weren't sure how to respond. The man dug around in the satchel that was next to him. He pulled out a small bag and handed it to us. Harry opened the drawstring bag, and we peered inside. The little pouch held a handful or two of coins and other little trinkets like small buttons and pins. Harry pulled the strings to close the bag and handed it back to the man. We thanked him but said we couldn't take the items. The man refused to take it back. He explained that he owned an antique shop in Flagstaff and the bag contained useless items that had been found with the pieces he'd brought to show our father. He was happy to be rid of the old coins since they were worthless and just taking up space." Her mug rose to her lips again.

Celia shifted in her chair. Was there a point to this walk down memory lane? Grandma's stories usually had one.

"So, did you take the coins?" Austin prompted her along.

Grandma leaned forward and set her mug on the picnic table. "Yes, we did. Later that afternoon, after the man left, we came up with a new plan. We were thrilled because instead of merely pretending, we now had something real we could search for. We took an old piece of canvas from our mother's art supplies and ripped it into small pieces. We each wrapped a few of the coins and trinkets in the material and tied it with twine. Our idea was to each bury our treasure, then search for the other's hiding spot. We were confident in our tracking abilities and that we could easily find the disturbed ground."

"Did it work?" Their game sounded like something she, Austin, and Luke would have concocted years ago. But she was still waiting for the moral of the story.

"Sort of. I was able to locate my brother's bag, but then our folks called us for dinner. The next morning, they woke us before dawn and informed us it was time to leave."

"So, your brother never found your hidden treasure." Luke nodded as if he had figured out the moral of this tale.

"No, he didn't." Grandma glanced down at her hands. "I've wondered if that pouch could still be buried."

Celia recognized the flicker of understanding in Luke's eyes. Too bad she wasn't a mind reader. She hated being left in the dark.

Luke turned to Grandma and leaned forward. "Is that what you were doing last night? Searching for the coins?"

Ohhh . . . Wow. Well, that explains a lot.

Grandma straightened in her chair. "I couldn't sleep and just had to check."

As Celia pictured her grandmother wandering in the dark by herself, sadness washed through her. "Grandma, why didn't you tell us? We could've helped you look."

Austin's unruly hair bobbed with his nod. "Absolutely. And we should tell Mom and Dad, when they get back."

"If you don't mind, I'd rather keep this just between us for the time being." Grandma looked down at her hands for a moment before continuing. "They've been overly concerned about me for the last few months, and I don't want to add to their worry."

Celia glanced at her brothers for their reaction. Without speaking, she was pretty sure they were in agreement. Mom and Dad did have a knack for overreacting. If Grandma wanted to keep it on the down-low for now, then that's what they'd do.

Hey!" Austin shifted to the edge of his seat. "Why don't we go check it out now? Do you remember where you buried the coins?"

Grandma's smile turned mischievous. "Of course, I do. I chose a very unique rock structure to bury it near so that I would always remember."

Well, what do you know? None of the scenarios Celia had conjured up in her mind as to why Grandma had been out by herself in the middle of the night came even close to this explanation. Sometimes truth definitely was stranger than fiction.

- - - X - - -

"This isn't a race, you know!" Mom called as the kids rushed ahead on the hiking trail.

Celia glanced back at her parents, who were falling behind the hurried pace set by her and the boys. Perfect. In order to discuss a game plan, the three of them needed to get away from Mom and Dad. She did feel bad for Siena, who was straining on the leash attached to Dad's hand, trying to catch up. *One of us should have taken charge of the leash.*

"Okay," she said to her brothers. "I think they're far enough back and won't hear us."

Austin rubbed his hands together. "Time to coordinate Operation Coin-Find."

"Operation Coin-Find?" Why did he have to be so weird?

"All covert operations need a name," argued her video game-obsessed little brother.

Celia glanced over her shoulder, checking once more on the parental unit. She waved her fingers at them, then faced the hiking trail ahead. "So, you've spent time thinking up dumb names, but did you come up with any ideas for how to actually find the missing coins?"

Austin bit his lip. He was so predictable.

Luke swiped the back of his hand across his forehead. "It shouldn't be too hard. Grandma is sure she knows where the bag is buried. Maybe while Mom and Dad prepare dinner, we can sneak away."

"What would stop them from searching for us?" Knowing Dad, he might try to ditch his domestic duties and hang out with them.

Austin kicked a stone, sending it skittering off the path. "Then one of us should stay back at camp and distract them."

Celia yanked on the sides of her ponytail, tightening it against her head. "I'll volunteer for that. Digging up dirt that hasn't been moved in sixty years? Not my idea of fun." She had a hard enough time growing her fingernails. Clawing through dirt was the last thing they needed.

"We need a shovel." Austin hopped around a large rock in the middle of the path. His hiking style remained the same as when he'd been little. The kid was incapable of walking a simple straight line.

Luke's phone dinged. He pulled it out and glanced at it, then stuffed it back in his pocket.

Avoiding Jenna's text again? Most definitely trouble in paradise.

Luke stepped over a small ditch in the path. "I know where the shovel is stored in the RV. You know Dad will head to the bathhouse after our hike. I'll grab it while he's away."

Who would've guessed Dad's insistence that they used the campground showers whenever possible, instead of the nice, private one in the RV, would help them out?

Austin jumped to bat a pine tree branch. "And while you're searching, I'll be the lookout and keep an eye out for the ranger."

"It's a solid plan." Luke stopped walking and reached his fist out toward them.

"Yeah, I'm diggin' it." Austin chuckled at his own joke as he extended his fist.

Celia responded with the same movement. A three-way fist bump sealed the deal.

Chapter 11

LUKE:
EXECUTING THE GAME PLAN

While Mom, Dad, and Celia prepared dinner, Operation Coin-Find began. Despite the idiotic, self-explanatory name, Grandma was thrilled with the plan. While Celia had the task of keeping the parents occupied, Austin stood watch along the path like a sentry from one of his games. Grandma directed Luke to the epicenter of the operation and quickly pinpointed the search site. Luke also put her in charge of monitoring his phone in case Austin or Celia needed to warn them of something. Hopefully, she was tech-savvy enough to handle the job.

The moment the shovel hit the dirt, any thought of a quick recovery was dashed. This was going to be a workout. The dirt entombing the coin probably hadn't been moved since Grandma had disturbed it sixty-some years ago. Seriously, digging through cement couldn't have been much more difficult than this. Oh, well, he hadn't had a decent upper-arm workout since they'd left home.

Grandma peered down at the dirt. "Oh dear. I hope the ground's not too hard."

"No problem." His muscles argued with the grunted response.

"Oh!" She held up his phone. "A message!"

"Is it from Celia?" Keeping Mom and Dad at the campsite could be the most unpredictable part of the operation. Plan B would be to test their improvisational skills.

"No. It's from Jenna. Want me to click on it and read it to you?"

Shoulda known. "No. Not necessary."

Grandma perched herself on a nearby boulder. "I've been meaning to ask you, did she like the postcard you sent her?"

He shoved his foot down on the shovel to pierce the dirt. "Actually, she didn't say much."

"Oh."

He shot a quick glance toward Grandma, trying to figure out what tainted that simple word. Disappointment? Disapproval? He was about to defend his girlfriend, but he realized those were his exact sentiments about Jenna's completely unimpressed response to the postcard. Sure, he was no Casanova, but receiving a postcard from your boyfriend had to be more romantic than an ordinary old text. While he'd pondered and stressed about the perfect words—the right touch of humor and romance—Jenna had only focused on the picture of the swirling staircase and stained-glass windows. Her only response had been something about how bad she felt that his family was dragging him to boring religious sites.

The measly amount of dirt he tossed to the side hardly counted as a shovelful. *This is going to take forever.*

"How is Jenna occupying her time with you away?"

The difficulty of Luke's digging task had obviously not registered with Grandma, who seemed thrilled to revive her relationship expert role. Or maybe, she was just taking advantage of the fact that he had nowhere to hide. She looked harmless, but underneath that sweet demeanor lurked one tough opponent. He took a deep breath. "Her usual stuff; hanging at the mall and the pool."

"I'm sure she misses you."

"Yeah, I guess." He jumped on the rim of the shovel, trying to force it to sink further into the dirt. There was just something about Jenna's responses that frustrated him—same with the texts he'd received from his friends, but he couldn't quite figure it out. Apparently, the consensus with his friend group was that poor Luke was stuck with his family on some lame trip while the rest of them were having the summer of their dreams.

He tossed the loose dirt to the side and jammed the shovel back into the small hole, with more force. Why should he be annoyed with their responses? After all, that was exactly his reaction before the trip began. They were only mirroring his feelings.

He glanced at his grandmother, perched on the rock, looking in awe at the beautiful landscape around her. Sure, he would've been having fun back home with his friends, but he'd have missed out on this time with Grandma, not to mention the amazing sites they'd seen.

He leaned on the shovel, giving his hands a break. "How do you know if you're dating the right person?" The words were out before he even realized he was thinking them. Oh well, he might as well let Relationship Grandma earn her keep.

Her eyes narrowed in concentration. "Your sweetheart should be someone you enjoy spending time with. Someone you can talk to about anything. They should appreciate you for who you are. And, of course, dating someone who can make you laugh is essential. Do you remember how your grandpa always loved to tell funny stories?"

"Yeah, kinda, now that you mention it." Grandpa had always made him laugh.

"They were silly, but they brought many a smile to my face." She got that dreamy look again. "Oh, and if a song he loved came on the radio, he'd grab my hand, and we'd dance around the kitchen while he serenaded me." She let out a little chuckle. "He wasn't a very good singer or dancer, but I loved those moments."

She rubbed her face like she was trying to wipe away the blush that reddened her cheeks.

Grandpa was a romantic? Luke turned back to the task at hand and plunged the shovel toward the earth. "That's a good list of traits." Sadly, he was not sure he could check off many of those items when it came to Jenna.

"Oh! She sent another message."

"I'll text her back later." The hole was slowly growing. No time for distractions.

She set the phone on her lap again. "But since you asked, I believe the most important thing you should consider when dating someone is if they share your beliefs and values. If you don't have those fundamentals in common, there really is no point in going out with them."

Values and beliefs? He was pretty sure no one in his sphere worried about those things.

"After all," she continued, "those we spend time with help shape who we are."

Hmm . . . never really thought about it like that. "Makes sense I guess." He couldn't help but think back to when he'd started hanging out with his football teammates. If he was being honest, the snide comments about the "churchy" kids at school had been part of the reason he'd stopped attending youth group. Mom and Dad had believed the too-busy-with-football-and-studies excuse, but he'd really just wanted to fit in with this new group. Besides, many of the kids his age had quit going. And just because his friends didn't go to church didn't mean they weren't good guys. He tossed away the thought along with another partial shovelful of dirt. "So, how far down did you bury this thing?"

She walked over toward him. "That's looking pretty good. I couldn't possibly have dug very deep."

"You're sure this is the spot?" What were the chances she actually remembered the exact location all these years later?

"Oh, yes, I'm sure. That rock formation is quite distinctive. I spent a long time deciding where to hide the bag so I would be able to find it again."

Another pitiful shovelful, and then he noticed something off-white amid the reddish-brown dirt. Could it be . . . ? "Hey, look."

She bent over. "That might be the material we used!"

He knelt and clawed through the dirt. The task was slowed by his trembling fingers. Could they really have just found the items Grandma had buried when she was a kid? He pulled out a small piece of canvas tied together by twine. He stood and handed it to her. "Looks like we did it!"

The look on her face was worth the blisters burning his palms. She carefully untied the twine and poured the contents into her hand. Out tumbled an old brass button, a small circular metal pin, some sort of cameo or pendant, a rusted key, and a few coins. Her eyes lit up as if the bag were glowing. "Let's go show Austin and Celia."

Chapter 12

Austin:
Challenge Mode

"I still can't believe you and Luke found it." Austin tried to concentrate on his video game, but even a zombie apocalypse couldn't hold his attention. His mind kept drifting to the coins. And to the conversation he'd overheard that morning.

Grandma tore her gaze from the red mountains that whizzed past as the behemoth rolled down the highway. "Yes, it's amazing, isn't it?" She looked down at her Bible which had been laying open to the same page for at least the last hour. She obviously couldn't concentrate, either.

They'd all assumed their usual cruising positions. Mom and Dad occupied the front seats. The front half of Siena's body and paws rested on the center console between them as she watched out the front window. The rest of the family sat around the table. While Austin attempted to play his game, Celia sketched in her notebook, listening to music through one earbud. Luke was doing whatever Luke did on his phone—probably texting Jenna, and Grandma had clearly zoned out, not even seeming to enjoy the oldies playlist she chose for today's journey. She usually tried to chat or get them to play cards while they were driving, but not today.

Last night, Grandma couldn't stop smiling like a little kid on Christmas morning. But today, the worry lines were back. He had hoped her secret hidden treasure was the cause of her stress, but finding it had only been a momentary distraction from what was really bothering her. And now he had a pretty good idea what it was.

While he'd been in the tent that morning, rolling up the sleeping bags, Grandma had gotten an unexpected phone call from her brother. Austin heard her answer and wander out of the campsite. While searching for some privacy, she'd stopped in the clump of trees behind the tent. Austin hadn't meant to eavesdrop but couldn't help but smile when she'd excitedly told Harry that they'd found the bag of treasure. Then her tone changed, and now he couldn't get her side of the conversation out of his head. With phrases like: "Oh, Harry. What devasting news," "Our worst fears," "All we can do is pray for a miracle," and "Keep me posted," he now knew what was going on. Grandma wasn't the one who was sick. Harry was.

She obviously wasn't ready to talk about it. And there was no way he could bring it up without admitting he'd listened in on her conversation. But there had to be some way to cheer her up.

"Where's our next stop?" He tossed his phone with the incomplete mission onto the empty chair across the way.

"Weren't you listening?" The exasperation in Luke's voice was practically palpable. "Dad only rambled on about it all evening."

Austin slouched down even further. "I kept tuning him out and thinking about Operation Coin-Find."

"The Grand Canyon." Celia reached for another colored pencil. "Remember? We're staying there a few nights."

Sounded vaguely familiar.

"Then off to my favorite of the parks—Bryce Canyon." Grandma continued to stare out the window.

A new idea popped into his mind—the Get-Grandma-to-Smile Mission. "Yeah, the Grand Canyon will be cool. I hear it's *gorges.*" He waited a beat. "Get it? Because it's a giant gorge?"

A perfectly delivered punchline deserved more than Celia's eyeroll and Luke's grimace. At least Grandma offered a slight grin. He'd classify that as mission accomplished, even if it had been a pity smile.

Grandma closed her Bible and patted her leather notebook. "Austin, I've been meaning to tell you, looking through my diary has brought back a lot of memories. I realized that my seventh and eighth grade years were actually some of my favorites."

"Seriously?" Would he look back someday and think favorably on this past year?

She nodded. "I'm not sure I realized it at the time, but life was much simpler before I went off to high school."

Now that seemed possible. His siblings had certainly changed for the worse.

Grandma placed the journal on top of her Bible, lining up the edges. "What are your favorite activities at school? Your dad said you were on the basketball team. I would've liked to have come to some of the games."

He squirmed in his seat with the memories of that disastrous foray into sports. "No, you wouldn't have. Since my school's so small, every boy joined the team, and we were terrible. In fact, sports really aren't my thing." His eyes darted over to see if Luke was listening, but his older brother appeared completely engrossed with his texts. He lowered his voice. "I'm not very coordinated."

Grandma's gaze shifted between her two grandsons. "I wouldn't say that. You maneuver around all the obstacles on our hikes with ease."

The little compliment made him smile.

"Which classes did you enjoy the most?" she continued.

"Probably math and science but I'm not really the best student. I don't get A's like Celia."

She brushed away his comment like a pesky fly. "As long as you do your best, that's what's important. God has different plans for each of us. Life would be pretty boring if He'd created us all the same."

If only his teachers felt that way and weren't always comparing him to his siblings. Luke was the athletic one. Celia was the smart one. Where'd that leave him? He wouldn't mind being the funny one, but no one seemed to appreciate his humor. His siblings probably thought of him as the annoying one.

"You know," Grandma said. "Your Grandpa wasn't the best student either. But his determination and work ethic got him into law school."

Austin tapped out a rhythm on the table with his fingers. "Is that why he didn't want people to know about his past? Because he tried to put it behind him?"

She nodded. "Charlie worked hard to change his life, and he didn't want people dwelling on his past."

"But it's cool that he changed. His story might have inspired others."

"That's what I thought. Of course, from the moment I met him, I knew he was a strong person with a heart of gold who believed firmly in right and wrong. It was clear to me, even if others couldn't see it. In fact, my father didn't approve of him at all. He continued to think of him as the rough boy from that picnic who had been accused of stealing. It actually took years for my daddy to see Charlie as I saw him."

"Really?"

She reached out and patted his hand. "You know, sometimes it's hard for others to see the change in us as we grow into the people we are meant to be."

He glanced at his siblings. *Isn't that the truth.*

She gave him a warm smile, then clapped her hands together, drawing Luke and Celia's attention toward her. "I wanted to thank you all again for helping me locate my missing treasure."

Celia pulled out the lone earbud. "Anytime, Grandma. I wish it weren't over. That little adventure was a blast."

"Hey, Grandma." Austin focused on her face, anxious to see her reaction to what he was about to ask. "I've been wondering, why didn't you want Mom and Dad to know about the buried items? Dad would probably think it was pretty cool."

Out of the corner of his eye, he saw Luke bob his head in agreement.

Grandma rubbed her hand across the cover of her Bible. "I'm not sure your father would have approved of us digging in the campground."

Luke slumped back. "Yeah, probably not. He is a stickler for the rules. Although, it wasn't like we were disturbing a national park or anything."

Maybe they were right, but keeping the secret was difficult. "Hey, want to play cards?" Maybe another distraction would keep Grandma out of her funk.

"You three go ahead. I haven't gotten through my daily readings yet." She pulled her Bible and journal closer. "Oh, before I forget, the verses I read yesterday made me think of you all. If you get a chance, you should read Ephesians, chapters 4 and 5. They spoke to me, and you all might find them interesting as well."

No one answered for a moment until Cool Hand Luke saved the day. "Thanks, we'll definitely check out those verses."

Austin held up the deck of cards. "While Grandma works on that, do you guys want to play?"

"Sure. Why not?" Luke tossed his phone on the bench.

"Okay." Celia boxed up her pencils. "But I get to choose the game."

Small price to pay, I suppose.

While Austin shuffled the cards and a '50s crooner serenaded them, Grandma began writing in her beautiful, slanted cursive on the back of a postcard featuring that amazing church in Sedona.

It was cool that Grandma and her brother were still such good friends. He snuck a glance at his siblings—who, for once, were not on their phones but spending time with him of their own accord—Austin for the win.

God, this has been such a great trip. It's so much fun hanging out with Luke and Celia. I don't want to go back to them ignoring me all the time at home. Please help this camaraderie to continue. Amen.

Grandma

Dear Diary,

The Grand Canyon is simply, well, grand. It's enormous! God, You did a grand job when creating it! (Get it? Grand?) Seriously though, I can't stop staring at it. Mama has found the perfect spot to perch herself near a scenic overlook. The last few days as she's painted the landscape, I've sat next to her watching her work. I wish I could create something so beautiful. But she says God blessed me with different talents and that I just need to figure out what those are.

I told her that even though I don't know what my talents are, I have narrowed down what I want to be when I grow up. As she continued working, I explained that it was between being an explorer or a detective, like Nancy Drew, because I want a life of adventure—just like our summers.

She actually set down her brush and looked me in the eye. That's when I knew there was something serious she wanted to say. I was expecting her to tell me those weren't good choices for a girl. But she said, "Gracie, marry your best friend and no matter where life takes you, it will be an adventure."

I'm really not sure what that means, but I just nodded and smiled. But maybe I can marry a fellow explorer or a detective, and we can work together.

Until next time,
Gracie

Chapter 13

Celia:
The Grass is Always Greener

A few hours and countless hands of cards later, they pulled into the campsite at the Grand Canyon, their new home for the next few days. Celia kept her outward non-caring composure but inwardly was psyched that they would be at this location a little longer. Based on the pictures she'd seen of the canyon, it would be another incredible place with stunning scenery. Her fingers itched to start sketching. But before they could go explore, Dad insisted everyone pitch in to set up camp. She doubted she was really needed, but to keep the peace, pretended to be useful.

"Celia, where you gonna sleep?" Luke unloaded the tent, where she'd slept with the boys again last night.

She hadn't planned on roughing it for more than one night, but the tent was the only place they had any privacy. Surprisingly, her desire to relive their roles in Operation Coin-Find had outweighed the need for a comfy bed.

"Umm . . . I guess I'll stay in the tent. It wasn't too bad." She'd forgotten that hanging out with her brothers could actually be fun.

Last night, they'd stayed up way too late laughing and sharing their roles in the adventure. Luke, of course, had performed the most critical role of digging for the coins, but she and Austin had had their own challenges. She'd enjoyed relaying in great detail how difficult Mom and Dad had been. For some reason, they'd been unable to work on dinner without stressing. *What happened to Grandma and the boys?" "Why is their walk taking so long?" "Do you think I should go search for them?" Chill, already!* Even after she'd pointed out that the boys had their phones with them and would call if something happened, they still hadn't let it go.

Of course, the parents had been worried about Grandma wandering off again. But still, talk about annoying. Kudos to Grandma for being right. If Dad knew she'd wanted to dig a hole in the dirt to search for something her ten-year-old self had buried there, he'd be convinced she was losing it. Quick thinking on Celia's part had saved the day and had kept her parents from searching for them—but it had meant she'd had to take one for the team.

First, she'd had to endure a step-by-step tutorial on Dad's secret baked bean recipe. Then when more time had been needed, she'd resorted to asking Mom about the friend she'd been in the movie with, Emily. When Celia had relayed Mom's response of, *"She was fun, but didn't always make the best decisions, so over time, Emily was someone I had to weed from my friendship garden,"* Celia had made sure to make it sound like some lame mom-ism, even though she hadn't been able to get the concept out of her mind since.

Austin had also shared his troubles during their operation. Turns out, the park ranger had shown up while making his rounds through the campground. Austin had managed to keep the man from stumbling across the archeological dig by feigning an interest in native plants. Thank goodness for the ranger's passion for plants and topography. He'd been thrilled to have a captive audience. Relaying the experience, Austin had made a huge deal about what a burden it had been, but Celia suspected he'd thoroughly enjoyed the mini lesson.

Celia placed the final folding chair around the campfire when Siena erupted in a barking frenzy. Two girls about Celia's age approached, and the goldendoodle added an aggressive tail-wag as she announced the visitors.

"Well, aren't you cute!" Siena was instantly enthralled by one of the girls with long, dark wavy hair, who bent down to pet her.

"We're set up in the next campsite," the other girl explained. A dark braid trailed down her back. She looked a year or so younger than Celia, while the one loving on Siena—most likely the older sister—must've been Luke's age. "I'm Mia."

"Hi. I'm Celia. You guys been here awhile?"

Mia stuffed her hands in the back pockets of her jean shorts. "Yeah, a couple of days. We're about half-way through our week-long stay."

Luke, having somehow set it up by himself, emerged from the tent. His eyes darted between the visitors, then settled on the older sister. As if she felt his gaze, she turned to look at him.

"I love your dog. She's so beautiful." The dark-haired beauty stood and reached out her hand. "Hi, I'm Britt."

"I'm Luke." He tilted his head Celia's way. "I guess you already met my sister. Austin's around here some-where. And the furball is Siena."

Britt tucked a strand of hair behind her ear. "Our parents noticed your family when you pulled in. They wanted us to invite you all to our campsite for dinner."

"That sounds fantastic." A break from their usual camping food would be greatly appreciated.

Mia shrugged. "I think our folks are anxious to find some other adults to chat with."

"We'll pass on the invitation and let you know." Luke's short answer somehow oozed charm, making Britt smile.

"Great. Well, hopefully, we'll see you in a little while." Mia pulled on her sister's arm.

"Make sure you bring Siena along. Our dog would love to meet her." Britt tossed the words over her shoulder as her sister dragged her away.

- - - X - - -

Celia was pretty sure onlookers assumed Mia and Britt's family and theirs had been friends for years. Turned out, the two sets of parents had hit it off immediately, and they'd all been doing practically everything together for the last few days: rafting, hiking, campfire talks with the rangers, games at night. The girls' dad had a guitar, and one night, they'd stayed up late, singing and laughing as they'd stumbled over lyrics.

They'd even attended Mass together at an adorable little church in town. Mia and Britt were fun-loving free spirits who were a blast to be around—a welcome break from her family's tiresome togetherness. Celia couldn't believe it when the girls revealed they hadn't even brought their phones with them on vacation after making a pact to leave them at home. Unimaginable.

They even had a buddy for Siena. Their German shepherd mix, Harley, was still a puppy and a ball of energy. One of her ears tried to stand tall like her regal German ancestors, while the other folded over, making her look like Scooby's little pal Scrappy Doo. The two dogs couldn't stop wrestling and chasing each other. At night, they crashed, completely worn out.

The only kink in the fun was that Grandma had been acting odd, especially the day they'd visited the west rim of the canyon. The two dads and Luke had been completely fascinated by the construction of the terrifying, albeit amazingly cool, visitor center and Skywalk. As the rest of the group had walked along the glass-bottomed, U-shaped, observation walkway that jutted out into the canyon, Austin had bombarded them with random facts about the canyon. Celia had attempted to remain as unphased as Mia and Britt had appeared. But when she'd glanced down to the plunging canyon below, her stomach had rolled in protest. Despite the fear, she'd had to admit, the view was breathtaking. But Grandma had barely seemed to notice. She'd briefly glanced around then told Mom that she hadn't felt well and needed to rest.

When they'd finally all taken their fill of photos and had been ready to leave, they'd found Grandma, looking rather tired and pale, peppering a park ranger with questions. Celia had been standing close enough to hear Dad quietly ask his mother if she needed a doctor. Celia had expected a snappy reply to Dad's overprotectiveness but instead, Grandma had sighed and said the only healing that would help her now was of a spiritual sort. Then she'd asked him if he would take her to visit the local priest.

After that, Grandma had insisted she was fine and perfectly content with the family spending time with their new friends. The extra time to rest, read, and pray had seemed to help, so Celia tried not to worry. Although, she knew she wasn't the only one with concerns. The rest of the family tried to be subtle, but Celia had noticed Austin, Luke, Mom, and Dad all sneaking extra glances at the family matriarch throughout the week.

Oh well. After tomorrow, it would be back to just being the six of them. Because, sadly, this was their last night there. After breakfast tomorrow, the two families would head their separate ways. Then they could spend more time with Grandma, making sure she was all right.

Celia's family would venture off to a new canyon. Although, she didn't see the point; no canyon could compare to this aptly named, massive hole in the ground. It was truly grand. Britt and Mia's family was scheduled to head back home to California. If only they lived in Colorado, then Celia'd actually have some real friends to hang out with. If only she could transplant those wildflowers to her friendship garden. She let out a little chuckle.

"What'cha thinking?" Austin broke into her thoughts.

Celia focused on the stars through the open ceiling flap on their tent. "Just looking at all the stars. Amazing how many more you can see outside the city." A partial truth. There was no way she was going to admit how sad she was to be ending their time here.

"Yeah, it's pretty awesome. But you know what I'm wondering? What's taking Luke so long?"

Guess it has been a while since he left for the community bathroom. "Knowing him, he found a rock to sit on and is watching the stars, too. I had no idea he liked camping so much."

Austin's sleeping bag rustled as he rolled toward Luke's empty side of the tent. "I didn't know I liked camping, either." His words softened and slowed. "Mom and Dad really should've taken us more often."

"We used to go a couple of times a year until we got too busy with activities." She tracked a shooting star across the dark sky.

Her brother's breathing deepened. "Night."

"Night." She pictured his eyes drifting shut.

Celia kept watching the stars. Maybe she could fuse the moment into her brain—a happy memory to pull out when she got back to her lonely life.

- - - X - - -

She was just drifting off when Siena's low growl caused her eyes to pop wide open. A moment later, the sound of the tent zipper announced Luke's return.

Instead of coming in, he just stuck his head inside. "Come on, sleepyheads, time to get up."

"What are you talking about?" Austin grumbled.

"I ran into Mia and Britt at the bathhouse. They want to show us something."

"Now?" She'd just found a semi-comfy position.

"Yeah, now."

She hated to leave her cozy sleeping bag, but no way was Celia going to miss out on one last adventure with Britt and Mia. "Okay, let me pull on a sweatshirt, but you'll all have to deal with my pajama pants."

She clipped the leash to Siena's collar, then she and Austin followed Luke. The dim beam of his flashlight led them to the rendezvous spot. The girls' silhouettes took shape as they approached. Harley yipped a greeting to Siena.

"Great, you got them both to come." Britt spun, her hair flinging over her shoulder, and led the group down a trail.

The canine BFFs happily trotted along, side by side.

Having been there for several days, Celia easily figured out that they were walking toward the canyon. Britt led them on a meandering path through pine trees and shrubby bushes. Celia's leg muscles felt the slight uphill climb. *Sure hope Britt knows where she's going.* Falling to her death by plunging into the abyss of the Grand Canyon would not be an ideal way to die, but at least her demise would have a cool story associated with it. Maybe then her friends back home would finally feel guilty about the past year. Doubtful.

Soon, they emerged onto a flat, open area.

"Ta-da!" Britt's sweeping gesture was caught by the beam of Luke's flashlight.

The view was spectacular, even in the dark. The scene before them was illuminated by thousands of stars lighting the night sky. Dark shadows shaded the deep crevices of the canyon.

"Wow." Not the most brilliant thing she'd ever muttered, but maybe the most heartfelt. There really were no words.

Britt lowered herself to the ground, lying back to stare at the twinkling night sky, her dark hair fanning out behind her. "Cool, huh? We came across this the first night we were here. I've wanted to come back, but there hasn't been a completely clear night again until now."

Mia sprawled out next to her sister. "Glad we could share this with you guys."

Celia joined Luke and Austin as they also lowered themselves to the ground. The dogs curled up next to each other.

"Isn't it amazing how many stars you can see out here?" Wonder filled Britt's voice.

"See that strip where there seems to be even more stars? That's the Milky Way." Mia lifted her arm to point at the sky.

Celia shifted to a more comfortable position, then located the spot in question. *Wait. You can actually see the Milky Way? Whoa.* She stared in awe at God's miraculous creation. "That's amazing. I've never been able to make out any of the constellations besides the Big Dipper."

"Yeah, me, neither," Mia agreed. "And how did anyone ever think the star patterns looked like a warrior or a lion?"

"It could be worse." Britt joined the conversation. "They were probably named by a bunch of drunk sailors who'd been out to sea for way too long. We're lucky they didn't name them after something they were craving."

The shadow of Mia's hand came into view again as she pointed to the sky. Her voice took on a low Irish brogue. "That group of stars shall forever be known as Bowl of Fresh Fruit."

"Aye, matey, and next to it is the constellation, Pitcher of Fresh Water," Pirate Austin added.

Celia pointed toward a line of stars. "Clean Shirt." She'd briefly thought of attempting a sailor impression but was too tired to try.

"T-bone Steak," Britt added.

"Flask of Rum," Luke contributed.

"Buxomy Maiden," Britt quipped back.

A giggle erupted from Celia's mouth. "With my luck, that would be my zodiac sign."

Their laughter soon quieted, leaving them to their individual thoughts. The whisper of wind and the dogs' heavy breathing were the only sounds in an otherwise silent night.

"If you could be anywhere else in the world right now, where would it be?" Mia broke the silence.

Celia smiled—easy. "Sitting in a café in Paris." A visit to the Louvre, followed by an afternoon walking along the Seine, then relaxing at a café to sketch and people-watch would be the ideal day. Celia had spent a lot of time this past year contemplating this—a sort of internal escape.

"Back-packing across Europe." Britt's answer came just after Celia's. She'd obviously thought about it, too.

"Scuba diving in the Caribbean."

Luke wants to learn to scuba dive?

"Riding in a jeep across the Serengeti in Africa," Mia stated. "Austin?"

Austin remained quiet for a moment, probably scanning the ridiculous possibilities zipping through his head. Something like visiting an alien world or searching for Atlantis. "Right here. Right now."

"Aww." When had her kid brother become so sentimental?

"Yes!"

"Love it!"

"Amen, brother!"

The collective response confirmed her suspicion that this moment was special to all of them.

Why couldn't life always be like this? Peaceful. Happy. Real.

Chapter 14

LUKE:
CHANGE-UP

"If you were a superhero, what would your superpower be?" Mia's voice once again filled the quiet pause.

Britt responded first. "I'd want the ability to fly, then I could travel the world."

Luke rested an arm behind his head. *Makes perfect sense. What else would a free spirit want?*

"That's a good one," Mia said. "Although, I'd choose the ability to become invisible. Then I could know the world's secrets."

"I think it would be cool to shape-shift and be able to look like anyone." Austin laughed. "Think how many people I could mess with!"

The kid is twisted.

"Time travel." Celia's voice sounded serious and wistful. "Just imagine getting to witness all the amazing times in history."

Luke watched the night sky and the millions of stars spread out before them. That one wasn't bad, but he had something even better in mind. "I would want to be Batman. I mean, who wouldn't want to drive the Batmobile?"

Britt nudged him with her elbow. "Such a guy response."

"But that's not a superpower," Mia argued.

"If I have all the cool gadgets, I don't need a superpower. After all, you can only have one superpower, but the possibilities for new gadgets are limitless." Let them argue with that logic.

"Then you can't join our little superhero crew," Britt responded.

"Yep." Celia agreed with Britt—of course. "Only genuine superheroes allowed."

"Geez, you guys are rather exclusive. Not sure I want to be part of such a clique-y group."

"Well, if you let us fly around in your Batplane, we might reconsider," Britt conceded.

"You wouldn't need my plane since you can already fly." *Two can play at this game.*

"True, but sometimes I just want to hang out with you guys."

He grinned, loving this ridiculous exchange. ""Hmm . . . well, I guess so. As long as you bring food."

"Pizza?"

"Deal." He extended his right hand toward her.

She shook it. "Then you're in."

The last few days had been just like this—full of silly, goofy moments, never worrying about saying the wrong thing or looking dumb. Why did it all have to end tomorrow? Maybe he could wish on a shooting star that the morning would never arrive.

Celia was the first to break the magical quiet that had descended on them like the peaceful night. "Sorry, guys. I'm starting to fall asleep. I better head back to camp."

No. Not yet.

"Yeah, we probably should get back," Austin agreed.

His siblings were such killjoys.

Everyone pushed themselves up except for Britt. "You guys go. I just want to stay a little longer."

"Come on, Britt." A slight whine tinged Mia's words. "I'm tired, but I'm not leaving you out here by yourself."

"I'll stay." The words were out before Luke thought them through. "I'm not too tired yet. You guys head back, and I'll walk Britt back soon." Whatever it took to keep this moment alive.

Mia bit her lower lip, then shrugged. "Okay. Thanks. I'll leave Harley here with you. Goodnight."

Harley whimpered as Siena reluctantly followed the other three down the path. *Can dogs miss other dogs?*

Luke laid back down and focused once again on the night sky. Harley curled up between them, resting her head on Britt's stomach.

"Thanks for staying." He could hear the smile in her voice. "I just want to soak this in for a few minutes longer. I'm not ready to head back home."

He rolled his head to look at her but could only make out the shadow of her face. "I know what you mean. It's so peaceful here." His gaze returned to the twinkling stars. "It's hard to believe I just said that. I did not want to come on this trip. At all. Now I don't want it to end."

"Same. I thought I'd be missing out on so much back at home."

The girl was a mind reader. "Yep. But now none of that seems important."

"Exactly."

He tracked a satellite moving across the sky. "My grandma told me that she always liked going on trips because it was a good time to reevaluate her life back at home. If there was something she dreaded going back to, then she would try to figure out a way to change it."

"Huh. I love that advice."

They were both quiet for a moment, lost in thought. *Why not open up even more?* "Yeah, but what do you do if it's your whole life that needs changing?"

Britt rolled on her side to look at him. Harley, losing her pillow, curled into a little ball. "Oh, come on. That can't be true. I bet you're popular. Celia said you're on the football team."

Starlight sparkled in her eyes.

"Does your life ever seem kind of pointless? I mean, I have fun with my friends, but everyone's so caught up in school. They act like our little community is all there is to the world." It was nice to have someone to voice this to. Grandma might be the relationship expert, but he drew the line at any self-help advice.

"They can't see outside the bubble." She let out a long sigh.

"Exactly." Finally, someone who understood.

Britt twirled a strand of long, dark hair around her finger. "I actually don't have a lot of friends at school for that very reason. They all want to focus on the next school dance, when all I want is to figure out how I'm going to have enough money to travel after graduation."

"To Europe? Were you serious about backpacking there?" It wasn't hard to picture this fearless girl visiting new cities.

"That's the plan."

"Your parents would let you go?" His folks would never agree to such a bold venture.

She turned back to focus on the stars. "Well, I have an aunt who said she'd travel with me."

"That's awesome." Maybe he needed some kind of goal to focus on, too. "So, what's your life like back in California? Bet you're a surfer girl, always searching for the perfect wave."

"Hardly. We live inland on a ranch."

So much for the picture he'd conjured up in his head. "Really? That's cool. Do you have a lot of horses?"

"Yeah. Horses, cattle, and goats."

"Is goat yoga a thing out there?" He chuckled. "My mom and her book club went to that a few months ago.

Seems like something that would've started in California." *Hope that quip doesn't offend her.*

Her laugh eased his worry. "Yeah, probably. Although, our goats wouldn't work well for that unless you want one falling on top of you. They're fainting goats."

"Fainting goats?" *She can't be serious.*

Britt pushed up and leaned on her forearm to look at him, her hair cascading like a waterfall over her shoulder. "You've never heard of them? If they are startled, they literally just fall over."

"No way! That's crazy." *Is she messing with me?*

"Yeah, it's pretty hilarious. Although, I can't always get them to do it."

"I'd love to see that." Still didn't seem possible.

"Tomorrow, before we leave, I'll write down your phone number and send you a video when I get home."

"That would be great. And I'll send you the pics we've taken of us the last few days."

"Thanks." She was quiet for a moment before adding, "I'd like to keep in touch."

Luke tried to swallow but his throat was suddenly as dry as the desert around them. "Me, too." *Most definitely.*

Chapter 15

Austin:
Real Time Strategy

The sound of the tent zipper jerked Austin awake. *Can't a guy get a decent night's sleep around here?* One eyelid peeled open. Siena lifted her head to watch Luke enter the tent.

"What time is it?" Celia's scratchy voice was a sure sign that she'd also been sound asleep.

"Sorry to wake you," Luke whispered. "I think it's after two."

"Two? Were you with Britt this whole time?" Celia asked.

Luke slithered into his sleeping bag. "Yeah. We were just watching the stars."

"Night." Celia rolled away from them.

Austin's eyelids had never felt so heavy, as if weights were pulling them down.

"Story time." Luke's deep baritone voice made him jump.

"Are you kidding? Now?" Celia flipped back toward them.

Yeah. Now?

Luke cleared his throat. "It's not really a story, but . . . well . . ."

Through the one eye that was currently cooperating, Austin made out Luke's form in the dim tent. His brother's arm was bent behind his head as a pillow, and he was staring up at the tent's pitched roof.

"'Well,' what?" Celia's calm tone shocked Austin. Pre-vacation Celia would have snapped at Luke for waking her. But this new-and-improved version seemed to recognize their brother's obvious need to talk about something.

Luke cleared his throat. "I'm going to break up with Jenna."

Silence filled the tent. Since Austin had never been a fan of his brother's girlfriend, he couldn't decide whether the appropriate response was to high-five him or offer condolences.

Celia lifted up on her elbow. "Because of *Britt?*"

Britt? Austin lurched up, his other eye popping open. "Wait. Is there something going on between you two?"

Luke let out a long, slow breath. "Yeah. No. Kinda."

Their normally articulate brother had lost all words. *Wow.* "Girls really are the root of all evil."

Celia whipped her pillow into Austin's head. "Why couldn't I have been blessed with a cool sister, like Mia, instead of smelly, annoying brothers?"

Apparently, not all of Celia's feistiness had disappeared.

Luke ignored the little dust-up. "I've actually been thinking about breaking up for a week or so."

Austin brushed the hair out of his eyes. "Why? Back at home you practically spent every moment together."

Luke huffed out a breath. "Yeah, I know. But I never realized we have nothing in common. Grandma has been slowly pointing it out to me, but tonight with Britt . . . well, it became obvious."

"You do realize Britt lives in California, right?" Celia asked the obvious. "You will probably never see her again."

"I know." Luke threw his head back on his pillow. "But for *three hours,* we just talked. Talked about our dreams, the stuff we love, questions we've always pondered about life. Just, stuff. For three hours." He lets out a heavy sigh. "Jenna and I have never connected like that. Ever since Santa Fe, I've been sending her long messages about the cool things we've been seeing, my fascination with the unique structures, and how I want to do more outdoors stuff when I get back. Her lack of response has made it pretty obvious that she really has no interest in any of it. While she's fun to hang out with, the relationship has no future. Breaking up is the right thing to do."

Celia rolled onto her stomach, propping up on her forearms. "I hate to be the voice of reason, but you can't be a Neanderthal and just ghost her."

"I won't just stop communicating altogether." Luke sounded so deflated; all the excitement in his voice just a moment ago—when talking about Britt—was gone. "But I don't want to be a tool and do it over text, either. I guess I'll have to wait until we get home. I just hate having to pretend things are fine when I answer her texts. That seems like a jerk move, too."

Austin rolled his eyes, even though no one could see. Luke couldn't really think that plan would work. "She texts you a gazillion times a day. How are you going to ignore that?" Note to self—*girlfriends are so not worth the headache.*

Celia sat up, pretzeling her legs in one swift movement. "I know how you could do it."

"I'm open to suggestions." Luke propped up on his elbow.

"You could tell her that the three of us made a pact to not use our phones for the rest of the trip."

"Like Mia and Britt." Would Jenna really buy that excuse?

"Yep," Celia agreed. "But we'd really need to do it." *Wait. She's serious? We'd all give up our phones?*

"I'm game." Luke's voice lost the despair.

"Me, too." Celia tucked a strand of hair behind her ear. "I can live without my music. What about you, Austin?"

The real question that was probably forming in her head was whether he could quit his video games cold turkey. Well, if they could do it, then so could he. "Yeah. Sure, let's do it. Operation No More Phones."

Celia shoved his shoulder but then held up her fist in the air toward the middle of the tent. "Then it's a deal."

"Deal." Luke raised his fist to hers.

Austin didn't join them. "Wait."

"Already having withdrawal pains?"

He ignored Luke's quip. "What about our cameras?"

Luke lowered his arm. "The kid's got a good point. I don't want to go the rest of the trip without taking photos."

Silence descended around them.

Celia chewed on her thumbnail, then raised her head. "Maybe we could borrow Mom's phone. She and Dad don't need both of theirs since they're always together."

"Good idea." They were back in business. Austin was the first to raise his fist this time. His siblings both added theirs. "Deal."

"Deal."

"Deal."

With that settled, they lay down again.

Austin buried his head into the pillow. This had been a great night. Happy dreams were sure to come. Luke's heavy breathing lulled him into complete relaxation.

"Confession time," Celia broke the quiet moment. "I never really liked Jenna."

"Me, neither," Austin agreed. "It's so annoying how her stupid purses always match her outfits."

"And they both match her shoes," Celia added.

"And her phone case," Luke quipped.

A moment of contemplative silence shattered when they all burst into laughter.

= = = X = = =

What were they thinking? What a moment of weakness. Austin glanced at the drawer by the sink where they'd stashed their phones, longing to implement a search-and-rescue operation. They should have waited to enact their pact until after today's long drive. As cool as the scenery was, colorful red rocks whizzing past got a little monotonous. What on earth did people do before they had cell phones?

A quick glance showed that he wasn't the only one feeling the withdrawal. Luke's hand kept drifting toward his pocket. Celia was busy sketching while humming a different tune than the odd choice of hip-hop music she'd picked for today's drive. Didn't really seem like her kind of music—maybe she'd chosen it just to annoy Luke.

The worst part was there were no distractions from their Mia-and-Britt withdrawal. The last few days had been a total blast, but now it felt like all the fun had packed up and went with the girls to California. He slouched down to rest the back of his head on the couch cushion and stared at the ceiling.

"Story time." Grandma stuffed her rosary into her sweater pocket.

Technically, it was more of a quiet pronouncement, which must mean her story was meant for their ears alone. *Fine by me.*

Having Grandma initiate a conversation was a huge relief. She hadn't exactly been herself the last few days. She'd insisted she'd been happy to have a few days to enjoy her book, but he hadn't been buying what she'd been selling. Did the others feel as guilty as he did for spending so much time with their new friends and letting poor Grandma fend for herself?

He scooched further up in his seat, and Celia set down her notebook.

When three sets of eyes settled on her, Grandma continued. "Thanks again for helping me find the buried items. It meant a lot to me."

"Of course." Luke's hand slid toward his pocket once again. He caught himself and placed his hands on the table, lacing his fingers together. "We'd do anything for you."

Her eyes lit up with a sparkly glow. "I was hoping you would say something like that. I wasn't entirely forthcoming with you."

Celia and Luke glanced at each other, then at him. Austin answered with a shrug.

Grandma's eyes darted toward the front of the motorhome. Presumably, making sure Mom and Dad didn't overhear. "Well, Sedona wasn't the only place that we buried coins."

"You mean there's more buried treasure?" A tingle of excitement slithered down Austin's back. *Was not expecting that bit of news!*

Luke leaned forward. "Did you hide some at Bryce Canyon?"

Grandma's smile—really more of a sly, little grin—smoothed out the worry lines that had creased her face for a few days. "Yep."

Luke rubbed his jaw. "Are you sure you don't want to tell Dad about this?"

"I'm sure." Grandma clasped her hands together. "This is our adventure. Any of the trinkets we find, you can keep as souvenirs. So, who's up for a bit more digging?"

"I'm in." Who needed to think about that?

Celia shook her head in disbelief. "Sure, I'm in."

Luke nodded. "Absolutely."

Operation Coin-Find was back in business.

Grandma

Dear Diary,

We are at the most amazing national park ever. Bryce Canyon is simply unbelievable! As we were driving into the park, it was raining. But the clouds blew away and it cleared up just as we pulled up to the cliff. We all four sat there and stared at the most incredible site—a double rainbow over this colorful canyon of the craziest looking pillars you've ever seen. I knew right then that we will be here for a while as Mama tries to capture the magnificence. No complaints from me; I think I could stay here forever.

And guess what? Daddy actually said we could use his camera if we promised to be extra careful with it. As excited as I am to try it out, it's probably best if Harry is in charge of it. I'm not sure I trust myself to not drop it in the canyon.

But that's not even the best part! Tomorrow, Daddy, Harry, and I are exploring the canyon on horseback. Horseback! I can't believe it! It's especially perfect because Harry and I have resumed our pirate game. Although, we changed it a bit because really, you never hear of pirates being in the desert. So, we are now pretending to be Old West settlers in search of gold.

Gracie

Chapter 16

Celia:
No Shrinking Violet

Celia flinched while Luke shook his head, determination in his clenched jaw. "No. Huh-uh. There is no possible way."

Celia, Grandma, Luke, and Austin stood at a railing, staring out at Bryce Canyon. Mom, Dad, and Siena were further down the path that rimmed the overlook.

Celia couldn't get over the beauty of the canyon in front of her. She'd never seen anything like these oddly shaped rock formations sticking straight out of the earth. The shaded bands of reds, oranges, and whites gave so much color to this valley of spires. Who would believe another place existed that could inspire her more than the Grand Canyon? God's creation was certainly spectacular, but she had to agree with Luke. How could they ever find anything in this mass of rock towers?

Grandma scanned the canyon. "Where's your sense of adventure?"

While Celia totally shared her brother's conviction that this appeared to be an impossible mission, the gleam in Grandma's eyes was hard to ignore. How can we disappoint her?

Luke motioned to the gaping hole in the earth. "You buried items somewhere down there sixty-some years ago, and you think we'll somehow be able to find them?"

Celia stared hopelessly into the vast, red abyss. "You're sure the bags are down there? Not at the campsite like last time?"

Grandma gave them a knowing look. "I'm positive."

Austin pulled off his baseball hat to scratch his head, then replaced it. "I'm confused. If your game was to find the treasure that the other one buried, why are the coins still here?"

Grandma wrapped her hands around the metal railing. "At first, we were disappointed that we never had a chance to find my hidden treasure in Sedona. But the more we thought about it, the more we liked the idea of someone, someday, discovering them. So, these bags were left on purpose."

Luke let out a low whistle. "And after all this time, your grandchildren might be the ones to find them."

"If they're even still here." Austin shifted closer to Celia as a group of tourists gathered to take photos of the canyon.

Grandma's grip tightened. "That's what we're here to find out."

"Grandma." Luke's voice took on his familiar, placating-the-parents tone. "You have a great memory, obviously. I mean, you were able to find the exact spot in Sedona. But this is a little different. How could you possibly know where to look after all this time?"

The mischievous grin that Celia had never noticed before this trip slid across Grandma's face again. "This time, I have photos to help us."

Three heads swiveled to stare at her.

Grandma bristled. "My goodness, it wasn't the dark ages. We had access to a camera. The photos were tucked inside the diary."

She could have led with that piece of information.

Austin dug his toe into the red dirt beneath his feet. "But all the rocks kind of look alike. Do you think the photos will even help?"

Celia watched the tiny dots of people moving around far below them. "And there are probably lots of different hiking trails that go down into the canyon. How would we know which one to take?" No way was their grandmother going to remember which path she'd been on all those years ago.

"We rode horses down. I bet they still use the same path for trail rides." Grandma dusted off her hands like that was the end of the discussion.

She was one determined woman.

Grandma turned her back on the canyon to give them her full attention. "Harry and I tried to find unique spots along the trail, where we could hide the coins. We chose sites near where our mother decided to paint. We were able to use our father's camera to take photos of the locations. So, I have three photos, one of each location. And, Luke, you will be happy to know that this time, no serious digging is required. The parcels are wedged into rock formations. You all are scheduled for a trail ride tomorrow. If you each take a photo, you can search for that specific place during the ride."

Easy peasy. *Not.*

Grandma must've realized that despite her reassurances, her accomplices remained unconvinced. "If you can't find any of the locations, then we'll tell your father, okay?"

"And if we recognize the spots?" Luke unscrewed the cap of his water bottle and took a swig.

"Then, we go back to see if the bags are still there." Grandma smiled, clearly aware that she'd won. "If God wants us to find them, He'll provide a way."

- - - ✗ - - -

Siena's low growl increased in volume the closer they got to the corral. The goldendoodle might be able to convince herself that she was tough, but it was highly doubtful that any of the majestic horses behind the fence found her particularly menacing. Her golden curls did not exactly exude fierceness.

Though she tugged Siena closer, Celia's focus remained on the dreamy, young cowboy leading a speckled horse into the corral. Light brown curls peeked out from beneath a tan cowboy hat.

"Talk about cute," she murmured to no one in particular.

"I couldn't agree more."

"Grandma!" Celia spun around, shocked by the comment, only to see that her grandmother's gaze was directed to an elderly cowpoke headed their way. "Maybe if you go with us on the ride, you could chat with him," she teased.

Grandma shooed away the suggestion. "I wish I could, but bouncing around on horseback doesn't sound like a pleasant way to spend the afternoon."

"Don't worry, Mom." Dad suddenly appeared behind them looking every bit the tourist, wearing a cowboy hat with his shorts and running shoes. "We'll take lots of pictures for you."

Grandma leaned down to pat Siena's head. "Siena and I will take a nice little stroll. I'm sure I'll see plenty of lovely scenery without aggravating my sciatica."

The old, weathered cowboy that Grandma had noticed finally reached them. "Howdy. I'm Mel. You must be the Webber family."

"That would be us." Dad reached out his hand.

He might be old, but the cowboy's handshake looked firm. "I'm glad you decided to join us today."

Austin slid in next to Celia. "It was a *spur* of the moment decision."

She jabbed her elbow into his side. Just one afternoon without a stupid pun would be nice.

Old Mel took Austin's dumb joke in stride. "Well, I'm one of the cowboys *saddled* with the responsibility to take you safely down the trail."

Austin's eyes lit up, thrilled to have someone play along. "That sounds mighty fun, *neigh*bor. Let's get riding!"

Cowboy Mel might soon regret awakening the beast. Austin's brain would keep churning out the puns now that he'd found a willing participant.

Mel's grin widened. "Hold your *horses,* young gun. Those who are riding can mosey along to the office over there and fill out some forms. We'll get y'all saddled up and on the trail soon."

Mom, Dad, and the boys shuffled toward the wooden shack that Mel's crooked finger seemed to be aimed at.

Celia handed Siena's leash to Grandma. "Are you sure you can handle Siena? I don't want her to scare the horses." *Or squirm loose and get trampled.*

Grandma's wrinkled hand grasped the leash handle. "Don't worry, Celia. I think I'm capable." She shot Mel a wink of amusement.

Mel leaned on the fence; his large hands grasped the top rail. "You have a mighty pretty name, Miss Celia."

"Thanks." She looked at him, trying to judge his age. "How long you been working here?"

He grinned. "You worried that I don't know what I'm doing?"

"Oh, no, sir. I was curious about the trails. My grandma rode a horse down the canyon when she was a girl. I'm wondering if we'll be heading down the same trail. I figure if you've been here for years, you might know."

He adjusted his cowboy hat as he looked at Grandma. "Is that so? Well, I do believe this would be the same trail."

That's a relief. It would make searching for the rock formations slightly more doable.

"However," Mel continued, "to answer your question, I haven't been working here very long. In fact, just a few years ago, I was the vice president of a bank in Houston."

"Seriously?" Hard to picture this man in a suit, working at a bank. His plaid shirt, worn jeans, and scuffed cowboy boots fit him well.

"That's so interesting," Grandma answered. "What made you change careers?"

"Basically, I woke up one mornin' and realized that I was not happy and not spending my days the way the good Lord would want me to. So, I made a change. Been here in Utah ever since."

Grandma placed a hand on Mel's arm. "It's nice that you were financially *stable* enough to make the change."

Grandma and Mel laughed. *Good grief.* Celia hugged Siena goodbye and left. She was not about to stick around and risk catching the pun-tagion.

- - - X - - -

The trail was spectacular, the weather perfect, and the sky an unbelievable shade of blue. Boss, the sweet horse Celia was perched upon, had the most beautiful chestnut coat. Before they began, they were instructed to ride single file as they made their way down the narrow trail. Cowboy Mel led the way, followed by Mom, then Dad, Luke, Celia, and Austin. Behind their family was a young couple. The way the guy kept fiddling with his wedding band made Celia suspicious that they hadn't been married long. Maybe they were on their honeymoon. And last, but certainly not least, was the super-cute cowboy. Turned out his name was Blake. Celia patted Boss's neck. Too bad the newlyweds and her little brother were riding between her and Dreamboat Blake. Was there a way to somehow change the line-up? Then the ride would be perfect.

Focus! Boy, that dreamy cowboy made it hard to concentrate on the mission. She forced her mind away from Blake and instead focused on the faded picture in her hand. The shape of the spire in the photo looked like most of the others in this valley. The photo was quite faded, but it appeared that the rock in question lacked the classic red color and was almost white. A somewhat unique feature, but still not enough to make it stand out. However, when paired with the arch directly behind it with the interesting bands of color near the top, it became a little more noteworthy. She scanned the area looking for those specific natural formations, but the literal search for a rock in a canyon was impossible. What had they been thinking? At least they could tell Grandma they had tried.

Busy scanning the terrain, she didn't notice Boss inching closer to Luke's horse in front of her. When his horse neighed in protest as Boss invaded his personal bubble, she pulled back on the reigns. "Be nice, Boss. Diamond likes his space."

Luke suddenly straightened in his saddle, probably about to go all Angry Bird on her for not being able to control her horse, but instead, he looked down at his photo, then back up again.

He sees something. "Did you spot your rock?"

He turned to look back at her, then pointed to the right. "Maybe. See those three spires clustered together?"

"Good eye." She snapped a photo of the formation with Mom's phone, then pinned the location on the GPS trail map. *Thank goodness for technology.*

Unfortunately, because of their search, the relaxing trail ride was not nearly as enjoyable as she wished it could be. This scenery was so stunning, and she longed to have nothing more to focus on than all the unique spires. Instead, she had to keep an eye out for one specific formation. Maybe she could hike back down here with her sketchpad when she was free to truly appreciate the canyon.

"Celia!" Austin called from behind her.

She shifted in her saddle to look at him.

"I have a tale of *whoa* to share with you."

She bit her lower lip to keep from grinning and faced forward. No way would she give him even a hint of encouragement.

"No, wait, I actually see something!"

She took the risk and peeked over her shoulder again.

"That rock there with the circular rings around it." He pointed to the right. "It's like a swirl. I think that one is mine."

She snapped a photo before marking the location. "Good."

Austin bent over in a slight bow. "I came; I saw; I conquered."

"Oh, get off your high horse and help me find mine."

Austin snorted a little laugh.

Darn it, those puns really were contagious.

She refocused on scanning the area. The boys had both found their rocks. Why couldn't she spot hers?

"Celia." Luke looked over his shoulder. "Grandma said she and her brother were set up at one location while their mom painted. So, the third rock has to be around here somewhere."

She glanced at the photo again. Maybe this spire wasn't right next to the trail. Grandma and Harry could have wandered off the path. But, just as Celia's horse rounded the next bend, she saw it. An odd white spire amid all the red ones. The unique arch perched in the distance.

"Got it!" She snapped a photo and marked the spot on the phone. They'd done it! They had found all three locations. Now came the next hurdle—finding a way to sneak back to explore them on their own.

When the caravan reached the bottom of the canyon, the riders climbed off the horses for a little break. The rest of her family decided to explore, but Celia stayed near the horses to spend some quality time with Boss. She stroked his shiny coat—what a beauty.

"I think ole' Boss likes you." Cowboy Mel strode up to her. "You spend a lot of time with horses?"

"No. We've only ridden a few times."

He checked the straps on the saddle. "You have a way with animals."

"I've always loved them." Lately, more than humans.

"Me too."

"If you love horses and animals, how did you end up working at a bank?" She ran her hand down Boss's silky-smooth coat.

He patted Boss's neck. "Good question. I've always liked math, and it seemed like an obvious career path."

"But you didn't like it?" Being stuck at the same mundane job for years, not doing what inspires you? *Sounds tortuous.*

"Ya know, it paid the bills and gave me time to be around my children when they were little. But as I got older, I realized it wasn't very fulfilling."

"It wasn't your passion." Boss neighed in agreement.

Mel shooed away a fly buzzing around Boss's face. "Well, yes . . . but not just that. At that particular bank, I was surrounded by people who didn't share my same values."

"They didn't 'get' you." *Oh, how I can relate to that.*

His eyes narrowed, forming little crinkles. "Yep."

"How'd you figure out what you wanted to do? Was it hard to make a change?" *Is it worth the risk to follow your dreams?*

"Well, I'll tell ya since you're asking. I was at work one day, stressed about getting some report finished, when a sharp pain traveled down my arm. I suddenly felt horrible and collapsed. Turns out I had a heart attack."

"Really? How awful." Poor guy.

"Actually, it might have been a blessing in disguise." He dug in his pocket and pulled out a sugar cube, which he offered to Celia. Guessing the sweet treat was not intended for her, she reached her open hand to Boss. They watched the horse enjoy the snack, and Mel continued. "As I was recovering, I realized that I didn't want to spend the rest of my life behind a desk filling out paperwork. I felt like I was wasting the gifts and talents that God gave me."

She thought of the skills she'd been keeping hidden from everyone. Could those be from God? Was she supposed to use them somehow? How do you know if He's leading you on a new path?

Mel caught her watching him. "Don't get me wrong. There is nothing wrong with working at a bank. You can help a lot of people to save and invest their money, securing a great future. I just felt like I had never used my skills and gifts to make a difference. I searched around for jobs and heard about this ranch. They were looking for a bookkeeper and someone who could help with the horses and head up trail rides for special-needs campers."

"That's so cool." If only he knew how inspiring his story was to her. But the old cowboy couldn't possibly understand the struggle she'd been dealing with for months.

He chuckled. "Convincing my wife was the tough part. But eventually, she warmed up to the idea. She was a schoolteacher, so she began tutoring at a nearby Indian reservation."

He was married. So much for a summer fling for Grandma.

He cleared his throat. "But enough about me. What are you hoping to do with your life?"

Great question. "I don't know. Some days, I wish I could become an artist, but that's probably not very realistic."

"The ideal goal, of course, would be to use your interests and skills in a job. That's not always possible, but you can always use them as a volunteer. I've found that the best way to find fulfillment in life is to help others." With a final pat to Boss's sturdy neck, he shuffled off to the next horse.

Hmm . . . Was there a way to help others through art or with animals? As she contemplated the thought, she settled on a nearby rock to wait for the others to return.

"Having a good time?"

Her heart lurched as she recognized Blake's voice. He *came over to talk . . . to me?* She shielded her eyes with a hand, and his handsome face came into view. His blue eyes mesmerized Celia like a hypnotist's pendulum. She couldn't stop staring into them. "Oh, um, yeah. It's amazing." *Stellar conversation skills.*

He grinned. "Where y'all from?"

"Colorado."

"That's an awesome state."

Her gaze lowered, and she stared at the red dust coating her shoes. Lately, everything seemed to be covered in a fine layer of red. *Come on, concentrate. When a cute guy comes up to chat, the least you can do is converse back.* She forced herself to look up at him. "Do you live near here?" *Oh my goodness. What an idiotic question. No, Celia, he lives in Virginia and commutes. Of course, he lives nearby.*

"Actually, I live in Nevada. I'm working here for the summer. My uncle runs the place."

Ha! Not such a dumb question after all. She ignored the dueling inner voices and concentrated on the cute guy standing next to her.

"That's so cool. Are you staying here in the park?"

"Yeah." He removed his cowboy hat to wipe his forehead, revealing unruly curls. "There's a lodge house for workers, so we don't have to drive in and out of the park every day. You guys here for a few days?"

"Yeah, a couple."

"The rangers put on some great evening events. There's actually a dance tomorrow night. Maybe you guys could come." He set his hat back on his head, covering those adorable locks.

She swallowed the huge lump that suddenly blocked her airway. *Did he just kind of ask me out?*

"All right," Mel bellowed. "Time to get a move on."

She flashed Blake a smile. "That sounds like fun."

"Excellent!"

How could one word turn her insides to mush?

Chapter 17

LUKE:
GOAL LINE FUMBLE

"Mom, are you sure you're doing all right?" Concern washed over Dad's face as the family walked along the road.

Grandma waved away his concern with a flick of her hand. "I'm fine. A nice evening walk is good for me."

"Yes, but it's slightly uphill, and I'm worried about you making the return journey after dinner in the dark."

"You worry too much." She turned and gave Luke a conspiratorial smile. He nodded his sympathetic understanding.

Grandma had been more energetic the last few days. The weight of the world seemed to have lifted from her shoulders ever since they'd agreed to help her locate the other bags. Relief flooded over Luke that they'd figured out what had been bothering her. *Thank you, God, that she's not sick.*

"We can always ask one of the rangers to drive us home after the show," Mom offered.

"Are we still talking about this?" Grandma snapped.

Luke attempted to cover up his laughter with a lame coughing fit.

Mom and Dad exchanged a look but remained quiet as they continued their trek toward the lodge for a chuckwagon dinner and singing cowboy show.

Luke glanced over his shoulder at Austin and Celia, sure they were as amused as he was at the exchange. But Austin was oblivious to the world, so preoccupied with scanning the views around him that he bumped into Celia. She nudged him, but the scowl and rude comment that would have been a sure bet a few weeks ago never came. She'd had a faraway look on her face ever since they'd returned from the trail ride. *What's up with her?* At least it was better than the permanent frown she'd worn all year at school. This trip had been good for his sister. The old Celia seemed to be reemerging.

Grandma wrapped her arm around his. "I haven't asked in a few days about Jenna."

He winced at the mention of her name. "Um, I actually decided to break up with her."

She squeezed his arm. "Did that decision have something to do with a dark-haired beauty?"

She really didn't miss anything. "Kinda, but it had more to do with you actually."

Her eyebrows lifted. "Me?"

"Well, your advice. I realized Jenna and I really don't have anything in common. Hanging out with Britt just made it obvious." Stashing their phones away meant he didn't have to deal with Jenna yet, which was a huge relief. But he couldn't believe how nice it was to be away from the group texts from his friends as well. Somehow, admitting the truth about Jenna had revealed how much he dreaded going back to the consuming status quo that had become his life.

"Did you ever have a chance to look at those Bible verses I mentioned?"

"Oh. No. Not yet." *Note to self—check them out for Grandma's sake.*

"Well, then do you mind if I give you a bit more advice?"

He grinned. Like he could say no. "Go ahead."

"Don't rush into another relationship. I'd recommend just being friends with young ladies and getting to know them that way. Dating shouldn't be for convenience but seeing if that is the person you want to spend your life with."

He was still trying to figure out how he felt about her old-fashioned advice as they rounded a bend in the road, and the lodge, Ebenezer's, came into view. The sweet, smoky smell of BBQ that had lured him along became even stronger. Luke's stomach rumbled as his mind focused on one thought. *These cowboys sure know how to cook.*

"Almost there, Mom," Dad announced.

Grandma leaned closer to her oldest grandson. "Like I can't see the enormous lodge in front of me?"

Luke grinned. "He's worried about you. It's sweet."

She shook her head. "One person's sweet is another person's annoying."

As they climbed the steps leading into the lodge, she gripped tighter to his arm. Dad pulled open the heavy wooden door, and festive western music greeted them, along with that mouth-watering aroma.

A teenage girl in a western dress and cowboy hat led them to one end of a long picnic table. A family with squirmy little kids occupied the other end.

Before his grumbling stomach disturbed the whole table, they were instructed to make their way toward the chuckwagon line for food. *Thank goodness for small miracles.*

Behind him in line, Celia leaned close. "Geez, save some for the rest of us."

He glanced down at his plate piled high with barbeque chicken, ribs, beans, coleslaw, cornbread muffins, and cobbler. "It'd be rude not to try everything."

Grandma stood at the end of the buffet line, staring at the drink station.

"Grandma, why don't I take your plate to the table, and you can get us both lemonades." Hopefully, it would contain more sugar than the batch Austin had attempted to make the other day—talk about sour.

Grandma handed over her plate of minuscule portions. "Oh, Luke. Thank you. I wasn't sure how I was going to manage my drink and plate." Unlike with

Dad's attempts, she didn't seem to mind help from the grandkids.

After filling her plate, Celia walked around him. "You look unbalanced. Let me help you with that." She reached over and snatched one of his corn muffins.

"Hey!"

She took a giant bite and grinned.

While the crowd chowed on the amazing feast, they were treated to a variety show by a group of cowboys. Armed with guitars and fiddles, they entertained the crowd with their unique repertoire. The funny cowboy songs particularly thrilled the little kids at the end of the table who showed their appreciations with out-of-sync clapping. Most of the crowd joined in singing the well-known country tunes. And surprisingly, the heart-felt religious pieces stirred an unexpected emotion within him. Between the melodies, the cowboys added their own brand of ridiculous humor. While the jokes could only be classified as dumb, Austin's deep belly laughs somehow made them hilarious.

Glancing around the table at his family, Luke couldn't help but smile. Everyone was so happy at the moment. No one was stressed. No one was in a hurry. No one was frustrated or angry. Instead, everyone appeared relaxed and having a great time together. If only he knew a way to capture this moment in time. He shook his head, chalking up the sentimentality to an overload of carbs.

After the show, Mom purchased a signed CD, then the family slowly made their way out of the building with the rest of the crowd.

Despite the darkness, it felt too early to head back to the campsite. "Hey, anyone want to walk up toward the main lodge? It's just a little further up the road."

Celia sidled closer. "Sure, I'll go."

"Yeah, we could get ice cream!" Austin had been obsessed with the self-serve ice cream machine since he'd discovered it after their trail ride.

"More food?" Mom held her stomach and groaned. "How could you possibly eat anything more?"

Dad glanced at Grandma. "Um, I think I've had enough walking for one day. I'm going to head back to the campground."

"I think I'll call it a night as well." Grandma accepted Dad's extended elbow. "I'd like to write Harry another update."

"Are you sure you know the way?" Mom's question seemed directed toward Luke.

"Mom, there's only one road. I don't think we could get lost even if we wanted to." Would she ever stop treating them like they were toddlers? Come to think of it, it was the same over-protective way Dad had been treating Grandma.

The corners of Mom's mouth pulled down into a frown. "I don't know . . . it's awfully dark."

Luke withdrew a small flashlight from his pocket. "This amazing new invention can help with that."

Mom sighed. "Fine. But don't stay out too late, and do not wander down any trails."

"We promise." Austin gave her a hug, which seemed to satisfy her.

"Goodnight." Celia walked off toward the lodge, dodging a tumbleweed that blew across the road. He and Austin followed before Mom and Dad could change their minds.

- - - X - - -

With ice cream cones in hand, Luke and his siblings exited the lodge and settled into wooden rocking chairs lined up on the wrap-around porch.

"It sure is dark." Austin licked his double-decker cone.

"I know. You'd never know there was such an amazing canyon out there." Celia curled her legs up on the chair.

The perfect opening to voice his thoughts. "That's what worries me." Luke turned to look at them. "I've been thinking a lot about those other bags. I can't come up with a way to search for them. I don't know if it's doable."

Austin lowered his cone. "But we've got to. For Grandma. She could use some good news."

Celia tilted her head. "What are you talking about?"

Austin let out a deep breath. "I guess with all the fun we were having at the Grand Canyon, I forgot to tell you."

Luke studied him. "Tell us what?"

Austin bit his lip as he gathered his thoughts. "I overheard a conversation between Grandma and Harry. I was right about there being some sort of sickness. But it's not Grandma. It's Harry."

Celia lowered her cone. "Are you sure?"

Austin slowly nodded.

Luke leaned back. "No wonder she was acting strange. They've always been so close." Poor Grandma. "I wish we could find the treasure for her, but I'm just not sure it's possible"

Celia's head spun toward him. "Hold on. What do you mean?"

He gestured in front of them, to the inky blackness. "Think about it. There is no possible way to go out there in the dark. We'd never find our way down the trail. And even if we somehow made it safely down, there's no way to locate those rocks in the dark."

"Last time we did it during the daylight," Celia pointed out. "Why can't we do that again?"

He shook his head. "I don't think that's possible here. That trail is busy during the day with hikers and trail riders. Someone would spot us and wonder what we were up to. I'm not sure what the rules are for venturing off the path." He savored a bite of ice cream while they thought about the issue.

Austin's face scrunched in concentration. "We could probably make up an excuse to hike down tomorrow. Maybe we could go before the trail gets too crowded."

Just as he'd suspected, they had not thought this through. "Dad wants us to hike with him tomorrow morning along the outer rim. We'd have to have a good reason to get him to change his mind."

Celia wiped the corner of her mouth with a napkin. "Why not tell him the truth?"

Austin licked around the bottom of his tower of ice cream, then shook his head. "Grandma didn't think

Dad would be on board with searching for the treasure. He'd probably say it isn't worth it."

Luke stared out into the dark void. "Maybe he would have a point."

"Are you kidding?" Celia looked at him like he'd lost his mind.

What is so hard to understand? As always, they were the dreamers, while he remained the logical one. "Think about it. We could get in big trouble if someone saw us digging around in the park."

"But we wouldn't be digging. Grandma said they were hidden inside the rock formations." Celia was so focused on her argument that she didn't notice the ice cream dripping down her cone.

Austin nodded. "We're putting things back the way they should be, back to their natural state by removing the bags."

Obviously, there was no changing their minds, not that he'd tried very hard. Truth be told, he didn't want to give up the search, either, but someone had to be the voice of reason. And as usual, that role fell to him. "Well, since you're not going to listen to logic, can you think of a time when we can get away?"

"After our hike tomorrow." Austin's satisfied smirk almost made Luke resume his half-hearted opposition.

Expecting Celia to continue siding with Austin, he was surprised by the shake of her head. "Tomorrow afternoon's no good. That's when we'll be getting ready for the dance in the evening."

"Why would it take more than five minutes to get ready?" He took a bite of his cone. *What is wrong with her today? She's acting weirder than normal.*

She crinkled up her napkin and threw it at him. "'Cause maybe some people don't want to show up smelling like a locker room?"

"Okay. Well, we could sneak out of the dance." That could be a great time to get away.

Celia squared her shoulders. "I actually want to go to the dance."

"Seriously?" His blatant surprise brought a flash of anger to her face. "You really want to go to a dance?"

"Why wouldn't I?" she snapped, Angry Celia re-emerging.

Like the Hulk, rage instantaneously transformed her. *Maybe that's what he should start calling her.* Nah, as fitting as it may be, he didn't have a death wish.

He was about to apologize but then wondered what he had to be sorry for. "Gee, I don't know. Maybe because you wouldn't go to one single dance last year at school."

The cold mask that he hadn't seen in weeks washed over her face. "That's not true. I went to the back-to-school dance. And besides, a square dance with my family is not at all like a stupid high school dance."

The fury in her eyes flashed at him like a warning shot. If he were smart, he would leave it at that. But he wasn't always known for his intelligence—that was Celia's domain. "Maybe if you'd gone to the dances or participated in some kind of activity, you would have actually liked your freshman year."

"Oh, yeah, 'cause hanging out with the cool kids is the only way to enjoy high school."

He ignored the obvious dig at his friends, not letting her avoid the subject. "Don't give me that. I watched you last year. You kept to yourself and tried to hide in the shadows. You can't tell me that isolating yourself was an enjoyable way to spend your first year of high school." This probably wasn't the place to bring it up, but frustration from walking on eggshells all year boiled over.

"Drop it." Her icy tone matched the chill in her eyes as she shut him out.

"Guys. *Please* stop fighting." Austin's earnest plea broke through the tension. "We've been having a great time together the last few weeks. Don't ruin it."

Fine. Luke shoved the remainder of the cone in his mouth and leaned back in the chair.

Celia's jaw clenched as she looked away.

Austin balled up his napkin and tossed it into the trashcan. "This is not about you guys right now. This is about helping Grandma."

Luke blinked and glanced at his little brother. He'd never heard Austin take charge before. While unexpected, the kid had a point. "You're right. Sorry I brought it up."

Celia didn't look at either of them but answered with a one-shoulder shrug.

Time to get back on track. "We still need to decide when we can go search."

Austin leaned his forearms on his knees. "There are only a few choices. Tomorrow is our last full day here."

He ticked off the possibilities on his fingers. "Either we go really early in the morning before our hike with Dad. Or we convince him to help us with our search. Or we could go after our hike, before the dance. Or we skip the dance and go when most people will be there. Or we go after the dance."

Luke contemplated the list of choices. "I don't see how we get away from camp before the hike, and telling Dad will end the search before it begins." He was about to suggest skipping the dance, but didn't want to rile up Celia again. "I vote for sneaking out toward the end of the dance while people are occupied."

"But it will be dark then," Austin pointed out. "As you said earlier, we won't be able to find our way."

"I guess there is one more option–going the following morning while Mom and Dad tear down camp," Luke suggested. "We could tell them we want to take one last hike."

Austin's right shoulder lifted in a half shrug. "That might work."

Celia shifted in her chair. "If we can't find a time to get away tomorrow, then that will be our plan."

"Deal." Austin reached out his fist.

Luke glanced at Celia before extending his. She still didn't make eye contact, but at least she added her fist to the circle.

Grandma

Harry,

We are in Bryce—it is even more spectacular than I remembered. Although, it is hard to focus on the beauty. You see, I have been avoiding writing this note. Our Grand Canyon stop brought the news we feared. Facing the truth has been crushing, but I can feel your encouragement to continue on. And as usual, you are right, there is no other choice. I just hope the outcome will be different. I pray for you each night, and know you do the same for me.

All my love,
Grace

Chapter 18

Austin:
Battle Plan

"Mom, can I look through your closet?" Celia posed the question the moment they entered the motorhome after returning from their hike. So focused on her mission, she ignored Siena's excited greeting. *Poor spoiled pup.*

Mom looked up from the card game she and Grandma were playing. "Um, sure. What are you looking for?"

Celia sailed through the camper toward the back bedroom. "I need something for the dance tonight."

Mom glanced at the rest of them. Austin was pretty sure he, Dad, and Luke all shrugged in unison. *Girls. They make no sense.*

"May the *quartz* be with you." Austin saluted as Celia departed.

"Austin!" Luke, Dad, and Celia's complaint couldn't have been more in sync if they'd practiced.

"Don't take my humor for *granite*," he replied. A canyon full of rocks had inspired a whole slew of new puns.

Mom looked through the cards in her hand and pulled one out. "Do you know when rock puns are the funniest?"

"Never." Luke opened the fridge and grabbed two sodas. Austin caught the can tossed his way.

"In the *Stone* Age." Her lips quirked as she laid the card on the table.

"Good one." Austin gave her an appreciative thumbs up, then took a long, satisfying sip. *Ahh* . . .

"Well, besides tolerating Austin's unappreciated humor, how was the hike?" Grandma slid a card from her hand and placed it on top of the pile between her and Mom.

"Exhausting." With a yawn, Dad collapsed into a chair.

Mom reached over and patted his knee. "Having trouble keeping up with the kids?"

"Nah. I just need a little nap." His head fell back as his eyes fluttered to a close.

"By the way, thanks for sending the lunch along with us. It was good." Austin had been starving halfway through the strenuous hike and had devoured the sandwich in record time. "What did you guys do while we were away?"

"We went on a walk with Siena. She was pretty sad that you left her behind." Mom scanned her cards. "Then we had lunch, and have been playing cards since then."

In other words—nothing.

Luke eyed the bedroom. "Let's see what Celia's up to."

Austin followed him into the small bedroom. They plopped on the bed and watched their sister pull items out of the tiny closet.

"What are you doing?" Luke leaned against the headboard.

"Finding something to wear to the dance." She held a checkered top against herself as she looked in the mirror. She examined the choice from a few angles, then tossed the shirt on the bed, landing it on Austin's foot.

With a little kick, Austin freed himself from the offensive article of clothing. "Can't you just wear jeans and a T-shirt?" That was his plan.

"No." She yanked open a drawer. Her eyes lit up as she pulled out a skirt.

"Is this supposed to be a dressy thing?" Luke took a gulp of his soda.

"Blake didn't say. I just want to look nice."

Blake? The cowboy? He caught Luke's eye. Suddenly, it all made sense. What was it with his siblings and their hormones?

"Blake, huh?" Luke's words were saturated in a teasing tone.

Celia rolled her eyes. "You can't give me a hard time; remember your little midnight rendezvous with Britt?"

Luke feigned indignation. "I would never give you a hard time."

"Right." She reached for two tops amid the pile of clothes on the bed. "I need a guy's opinion. Which one do you prefer?" She held them up for evaluation.

Austin glanced between the blue one with white lacy stuff around the collar and the plaid one with rhinestone buttons. There must be a right choice, but he had absolutely no idea what it would be. It didn't matter. Either shirt would be better than the black and gray his sister had worn all year. Although, during this trip, her wardrobe had received a much-needed mini makeover. The shades of depressing had been replaced by more colorful souvenir T-shirts.

He tried to read his sister's anxious expression as she waited for an answer. He took a drink as he contemplated his next move. Saying the wrong thing could make annoyed-Celia appear, and he'd been trying to avoid his sister's evil alter ego at all costs. Was it always like walking through a minefield when dealing with girls? Her imploring gaze didn't shift from his face. Finally, he figured the best answer was a shrug.

She huffed and rolled her eyes, then turned her attention to Luke.

He pointed at the lacy collar number. "Definitely the blue one. It brings out your eyes."

Her mouth dropped open, but she snapped it shut in a hurry. "Oh. Uhm . . . thanks." She dropped the plaid one and looked closely at the blue top.

"It's good to see you excited about this." Luke swirled his soda.

She jutted out her chin. "Just because I didn't want to go to the stupid school dances doesn't mean I don't like to dance."

Oh, great. Not this again. Austin lifted his soda can for another drink.

Luke held up a hand in surrender. "I didn't mean anything by it."

She turned her back on her brothers—her signature way of ending a conversation—and began hanging the discarded choices back in the closet. *Guess we have been dismissed.*

Reading the not-so-subtle hint, Luke stood and walked toward the door. "Hey, you should wear your hair up in one of those messy buns."

Celia froze and turned to watch him leave. A small smile slid across her face.

Well played, big brother. Well played.

- - - X - - -

With Celia probably fussing with her hair, Mom and Grandma still playing cards, Dad napping, and Luke doing who knew what, Austin decided to take Siena on a walk to the overlook at the edge of the campground. His first impulse was to waste time playing a video game, but since that wasn't a possibility, a walk would have to do.

Siena happily led the way through the campground. Her tail wagged in delight as they passed the RVs, pop-up campers, and tents. Her ears perked up at the laughter coming from one of the sites. Were all those families having a good time? Did they all get along? Did any of them argue like he and his siblings?

A boy and his dad walked by, fishing poles in hand. Austin returned the boy's wave. Could any of these vacationers be wondering how to change their lives? Over the last few days, Austin had tried to figure out how to implement a strategic battle plan to make things better at home. But how could he change the way his family saw him? How could he make his teachers get to know him instead of comparing him to his siblings? How could he get people to see that he wasn't just a little kid anymore? If only Grandpa were still around to offer words of advice on how he had done it.

Dear Lord, sometimes I feel so alone. Like no one understands me. I mean, I know You do, but why can't anyone else? I don't feel comfortable opening up to my friends or Mom and Dad. And there's no way I can tell any of my teachers or siblings since they're the problem. Maybe Grandma would get it, but she seems to have so much on her mind right now. All I have is You. Please show me the way. Amen.

Siena yanked so hard on the leash that it almost slipped out of his hand as he was ending his prayer with a sign of the cross. He looked up from the dirt path he'd been focused on to see Luke perched on a bench at the overlook, staring out at the unique alien-looking rocks of Bryce Canyon. Luke glanced over at Austin and Siena, probably assuming they had followed him.

"Sorry. Didn't know you were here. I'll leave." Better to set the record straight before big bro got mad.

Luke patted his leg for Siena to join him. "Nah. It's okay. I was trying to figure out a plan for tonight."

Grandma's treasure. Austin hadn't thought about them all day. *Guess I was too distracted with the rock jokes rolling around in my brain.* A giggle bubbled its way up. *Hey, good one!* He resisted the urge to share his newest *nugget* with Luke since his brother had no appreciation for the genius of puns. Instead, he sat on the bench watching two chipmunks who seemed to be playing tag. "Come up with anything?"

Luke shifted to give him room. "Nothing new."

"Guess Celia won't be any help since she'll probably be hanging out with Blake the whole night." *Still can't believe she's into the cowboy.* But it was better than her sulking around.

Luke's eyes squinted as he surveyed the canyon. "Hmm . . . maybe we can use that to our advantage."

Austin dug his toe into the dirt. "How so?"

"Yeah, how so?" asked a new voice. The brothers turned to see Celia standing behind them, her hands on her hips. "Talking about me, I see."

Thought she was getting ready.

Luke gave her a head bob in greeting. "I was just thinking we could use your date with Blake as a distraction."

"It's not a date." She sat next to Austin, then scooched away. "Eww . . . you need a shower before tonight."

Ignore her. You probably don't smell that bad. Although, a quick shower might not be the worst idea ever. "What's your plan, Luke?"

His older brother leaned forward, arms resting on his knees, and turned his head to look at them. "Well, Mom and Dad will be so focused on what's going on between Celia and Blake that they won't even notice if you and I sneak out to hunt for the coins."

"So, the two of us have to go searching in the dark by ourselves?" Visualizing this idea conjured up all kinds of creepy possibilities. *What kind of wild critters are down there?*

Luke nodded. "Yeah. It should be a good time since most people will presumably be at the dance. Of all the possibilities, it seems like the best option."

The plan was solid. But the unknowns of the canyon kept swirling through Austin's head. His shoe connected with a small rock, sending it hurtling toward the railing, causing the chipmunks to scurry away. "I hope we don't get lost."

"There might be another way." Celia bit her thumbnail and looked out at the scenery. She turned to look at them, brushing a strand of hair off her face. "Blake would know the trail much better than we do. What if we ask him to help us? I bet he'd jump at the chance for an adventure."

An expert with them in the canyon—excellent idea.

Austin rotated his head to gage Luke's reaction. *Please, like it.*

Luke's eyebrows pinched together as he contemplated the suggestion. "Going with him would make the job easier." He rubbed his hand along his jawline. "Why don't you ask him and see what he says? If he's not interested, then Austin and I will go by ourselves."

Hopefully, Blake would be up for an adventure because, as far as Austin was concerned, the thought of hiking down into the canyon by themselves was terrifying.

Chapter 19

Celia:
Red Carpet Treatment

"Celia!" Dad's voice dripped exasperation. "The dance will be over by the time we get there."

"I'm ready!" After one last look in the mirror, she exited the small RV bathroom.

"Finally," Austin mumbled.

The family hadn't moved from their card playing positions since she'd holed herself away to prepare for the evening. As they turned toward her, stunned silence suddenly filled the space.

"What?" The word came out a little more aggressively than she'd intended. She'd expected some kind of reaction, but not this roomful of surprised emoticons staring at her. *Maybe this was a mistake.* She glanced

behind her, ready to dart back into the bathroom to change.

Mom, the mind reader, jumped out of her seat and rushed over. "You look absolutely beautiful."

"W—wow," Dad managed to sputter.

She glanced down at her outfit. A denim skirt and the blue shirt she'd found in Mom's closet hardly seemed that amazing.

"I thought you said we didn't have to dress up." Austin flicked some dirt off his jeans.

Luke's eyebrows raised. "I think you will definitely get Blake's attention."

Dad's head whipped his way. "Blake? Who's Blake?"

Grandma reached over and patted her son's hand. "That cute cowboy from the trail ride."

"What?" Dad's panicked gaze fell on Mom, who shrugged. He turned his attention back to Celia. "You have a *date?*"

Her cheeks burned. *Luke is a dead man.* Why had she decided to try and look cute? It was so not worth this third degree. "No. I don't have a date."

"Date or no date, you look lovely." Mom shot Dad a pointed look.

Dad's brows furrowed, then he took a deep breath. "Yes, you do. You look . . . perfect."

"Well, come on. What are you all waiting for? We're going to be late." Celia marched toward the door. *What a bunch of weirdos.*

- - - X - - -

Country music wafted through the air as they neared the barn. Celia quickly scanned the area, anxiously searching for her cowboy. The majority of the large space was set up as a dance floor. Food and beverage stations lined either side of the huge barn doors. Tables and chairs occupied the opposite wall. The cowboy band from the other night provided the music on a stage to the right.

Most everyone was dressed casually, which made sense. Who would think to bring nice clothes on a trip to a national park? Celia suddenly regretted her choice of outfits until her gaze fell on Blake across the barn. In dark jeans, cowboy boots, and a white button-down shirt that highlighted his bronzed skin, he was breath-takingly handsome. As if sensing her presence, he looked her way and actually did a double take. His eyes lowered in a quick scan before locking onto her gaze. A smile spread across his cute face. *Okay, that was worth all the effort.* Despite her family's humiliating reaction.

Blake strode toward her, like some kind of movie-moment. As he neared, her heartrate quickened. *Oh my gosh, he's amazing.* Out of the corner of her eye, she spied Mom pulling Dad toward the far side of the room. *Thanks, Mom.*

"Hmm." Grandma squeezed her arm. "He certainly cleans up nicely."

Luke leaned close. "Told you to wear your hair up."

He flinched as her elbow jammed into his side.

"Don't forget to see if he'll help us." Austin tossed out the reminder before the three of them thankfully walked away.

And then Blake was suddenly beside her, open admiration in his gaze. "Celia. I'm so glad you came."

"Of course. It sounded fun."

His head tilted toward the dance floor, those soft curls shifting with the movement. "Do you want to dance?"

She watched the crowd, their movements synchronized unison. "Um. I don't really know how to dance to country music."

He grinned. "I bet you'll catch on to the line dances quickly. Come on." He held out his hand.

As she placed her hand in his, a shiver coursed through her. "Sure."

He eased his way into the middle of the crowd, and they joined a line of dancers. *Why didn't I ever learn to line dance?* She concentrated on the moves, and before long, she was clapping, hopping, swaying, and turning with the rest of the group, who seemed to have been doing these same dances for years. Anytime she or Blake missed a move or bumped into another dancer, they'd laugh, then join back in.

Despite the mistakes, they were much more in sync that Mom and her partner. Dad, who kept turning the wrong way and was completely unable to master the routine, eventually waved her off. But Luke and Austin came to the rescue and flanked Mom for the rest of the dance. *How do they know how to do this?*

During a slide step to the left, she glanced at Blake and found him smiling at her. A nervous giggle trickled up her throat like effervescing bubbles. "What? Am I terrible?"

His smile widened. "No. You're great." He leaned close to her. "Do you know how cute you are when you're concentrating?"

Thank goodness for the warm room and the exertion from dancing. Maybe her already red cheeks camouflaged her blush. She usually hated how flushed her cheeks became but, at the moment, was thankful for the annoying trait. "I bet you say that to all the girls." *Is she really flirting with this adorable cowboy?*

"I'm surprised you've never line danced before. I'd think country music would be big in Colorado."

She concentrated on the two steps forward, then back. "Luke's a fan, but honestly, it was never my favorite." County music might be popular with her classmates, but she'd never made it through one high school dance, so she didn't know—a fact she was not sharing with him.

Nope. Stop. You're not ruining this evening with that thought. She snuck another peek at her handsome dance partner. Too soon, the song ended, and everyone applauded.

She turned to walk off the dance floor as the band started a slower song. Blake's warm hand latched on her arm.

She turned to look at him, fluttering butterflies made it hard to breathe.

"May I have this dance?" The hopeful look in his eyes stole her remaining breath.

Feeling like Cowgirl Cinderella at the hoedown, Celia placed her hand in his. She tried to remember how to breathe normally as he placed his other hand on her waist. Gathering courage, she leaned a little closer to him. "Can I tell you a secret?"

His eyebrows arched. "This could be interesting. Go ahead."

Her heartrate increased as she leaned in so he could hear her whisper. "I don't really know how to dance like this, either." Somehow, being there, where no one knew her except for her family, made her self-consciousness disappear.

His eyes crinkled at the edges. "You don't have to do anything but follow along and let me lead."

With no idea what that even meant, she focused on letting him take charge as they moved around the dance floor.

The movement, the music, the dancing partner—it was all so perfect. A happy warmth filled her. *Thank you, God, for this one perfect moment.*

His head lowered, and his breath warmed her neck, instantly increasing her body temperature. "I don't think your brother likes me very much."

She pulled back at the unexpected comment. Her gaze moved to the side of the room, where Austin stood like a gladiator, arms crossed, fiercely staring at them. *Can't he let her enjoy the moment?*

Their mission came to mind, and she sighed. "It's not that. He wants me to ask you something."

Blake's curls slid across his forehead as his head tilted to the side. "Oh? What's that?"

"Um . . . it's a little complicated."

He winked. "Well, this is sounding more and more intriguing." He dropped his hand from her waist, then raised their clasped hands to spin her.

Another giggle escaped.

While the final notes of the song filled the air, he pulled her close. He slid his forearm along the small of her back, then leaned her back for a dip. Her heart pounded against her chest.

When he eased her up, a mischievous smile crossed his face.

As the crowd applauded the band, he squeezed her hand. "Let's go get some air."

She hated leaving the dance floor but followed him out the large barn doors to a bench under a towering tree. The cool night air felt so refreshing after the warmth of the crowded barn.

Unsure how to act, she sat on the bench and clasped her hands in her lap. "That was so much fun. You're a great instructor."

He joined her on the bench, remaining at a respectable distance. "It's easy when you have an amazing partner."

Blake most likely flirted with lots of girls, but tonight, she didn't care. Tonight, she was determined to enjoy the attention.

"So, what does your brother want you to ask me?" He leaned back resting his arm along the back of the bench.

She contemplated scooching closer so his extended arm could drape over her shoulder. The mere thought made her cheeks burn, so instead she kept her eyes lowered and fiddled with the hem of her skirt. "Well, it's more like a favor."

She could feel his gaze as he waited for her to continue.

Confident her blush had subsided, she glanced around to make sure there were no eavesdroppers. "Would it be possible for you to help us go down the trail tonight?"

His eyebrows furrowed. "Why?"

"Before I explain, please feel free to say no. I don't want you to get in trouble or anything." She took a deep breath, then proceeded to tell him the whole story of how, decades ago, her grandma and great-uncle had hidden items within the rock formations.

His eyes intently watched her. "That's why you kept taking photos of certain formations during the trail ride."

She nodded. "Yep. We're scheduled to leave Bryce tomorrow afternoon." Saying the words caused a wave of sadness to crash down, threatening to drown her happiness. She shook it off. *No time for regret.* "We promised our grandma we would search before we leave. Tonight seems like the only possibility. But we're afraid of getting lost in the dark."

"So, you figured going with a guide would help."

She grimaced. *Please don't think that was the only reason I wanted to spend time with you.*

His eyes squinted into the fading light. Finally, he grinned. "Let's do it."

"Really?" She'd hoped that would be his response, but hearing the words still came as a surprise.

He ran a hand through his curls. "Yeah, why not? I could use an adventure. Why don't you get your brothers and meet me back out here in twenty minutes?"

She stifled the desire to wrap her arms around him in a hug. "Okay." Too bad she couldn't spend her last evening here at Bryce alone with Blake instead of having her brothers tag along. But at least she'd always have the memory of that dance.

Grandma

Harry,

You have no idea how much I wish you could be here. This place is rejuvenating my soul. While I may have had ulterior motives for the trip, it really is making a difference. They needed this. And I have reason to be hopeful that the pieces to our plan are falling into place. I can hear you now—have faith; all will work out as it is supposed to.

I miss you.

Grace

Chapter 20

LUKE:
FOURTH AND INCHES

Luke's insides churned as he waited for Celia. *What is taking so long?* It seemed like an eternity since she and Blake had walked out of the barn. *What if Blake won't help? Do the three of them attempt the plan alone, or wait until morning?*

Just as he was about to go searching for them, Celia appeared near the main entrance of the barn—although it took Luke a moment to recognize her. He still wasn't used to her new look. When their eyes met, she motioned him over. He nudged his foot-tapping brother to follow. Time to find out what Blake had to say.

"Well?" Luke asked when they reached Celia.

Her smile released the knot in his stomach. "He'll do it. We're supposed to meet him out by the trailhead in twenty minutes."

"Good." They were in business. He turned to Austin. "Tell Mom and Dad that Blake is going to show us something and that we'll be back later." He debated telling Grandma the truth, but she probably wouldn't like them going down in the dark. Besides, surprising her later this evening would be fun.

Ten minutes later, they were off to meet Blake. The dance music faded as they rounded the corner of the barn and found him waiting, leaning against a black four-wheeler.

As they approached, their cowboy friend grinned, but his eyes were only on Celia. Luke glanced at her.

The way they were smiling at each other, he and Austin might as well have been invisible. Normally, he wouldn't have appreciated being ignored, but tonight, seeing his sister happy was worth the brush-off.

Austin ran toward the four-wheeler. "Are we taking this down?"

Blake tapped the side of the vehicle. "Yep. Hiking down would take too long, and I wouldn't want to lead the horses in the dark. My uncle lets me borrow this all the time, so we're good to go."

Austin perched himself in the passenger seat. "Time for Operation Coin-Find 2.0."

One of Blake's eyebrows arched.

Celia latched onto Austin's sleeve and yanked him out of the seat. "Ignore Austin," she told Blake. "We do." She slid onto the vacated seat.

Austin shot Luke an annoyed look.

He really thought he'd get to ride shotgun? Luke gave his little brother a visual warning with the shake of his head. This definitely was not the time for sibling squabbles. Austin reluctantly joined Luke on the back of the ATV. They stood on the bumper and hung onto the roll bar, ready for whatever lay ahead.

Blake slid into the driver's seat, and Celia pulled up the GPS app on Mom's phone. They huddled together as she showed him the pinned locations.

"Here's where the formations are located." She tucked a loose strand of hair behind her ear.

"Okay." Blake pointed to one of the marked areas. "We'll begin with the closest one and work our way down." A flick of his wrist brought the engine to life. "Let's roll."

Celia and Blake chatted and laughed as they traveled down the trail. You'd think they were on a date. *Guess maybe they are.*

"She sure acts different with him," Austin whispered the obvious.

"That's for sure." He grinned at his kid brother. "Kinda nice, huh?"

The further they descended into the canyon, the darker it became. Luke clung tighter to the roll bar as the vehicle pitched over rocks on the steep path. As the moon rose, dark shadows of the odd, rocky formations loomed around them. Hopefully, they could find the correct spots in the dark. If not, they'd have to change the game plan.

Eventually, the four-wheeler stopped. The brothers hopped off the back, then Luke flipped on his flashlight to scan the area, getting reacquainted with the canyon. This first formation was the one he had the photo of and had been tasked to find.

"I think it was this way." Feigning more confidence than he felt, Luke veered off toward the left. The others followed along.

This formation was a good one to start with, being the closest to the trail and most recognizable. Luke guessed they only needed to walk about twenty yards to get to their destination. As he walked, the disconcerting rustling and chirping noises of unknown origin made him thankful to have company. What kind of creatures lurked in the darkness? He continued his search and breathed a sigh of relief when his flashlight beam illuminated a familiar-looking formation. He strode toward it, hoping it was the right one. In the dark, the rocky spires all tended to look alike.

"You really think something is hidden in this?" Blake's voice held a definite note of skepticism.

"Yeah." Celia slowly walked around the clump of three spires. "When we were in Sedona, we found the first bag right where Grandma said it would be."

Luke studied the natural structure. The center rock, which reached higher toward the dark sky, had a distinctive flat top. Yep, this was the one. Now, where would Harry and Grandma have hidden the bag? *Think like a kid.*

Celia yanked the flashlight out of his hand and aimed it at her notes. "Okay. Grandma said this one is wedged between two of the spires."

He held out his hand until she relinquished the flashlight. It was too dark to know for sure, but he imagined an eye roll accompanied the hand-off. He moved closer to the rocks to continue his survey and shone the light into the space where the spires joined together.

"See anything?" Austin asked.

"Not really."

"Think about all the wind and rainstorms that have happened since she placed it there. We need to brush away some of the dust." Celia dug around in her backpack and pulled out a paintbrush. "Try this."

Decent point. He handed the flashlight to Austin, then brushed away red dust like his archeologist great-grandpa might have done. Amazing how much loose sediment had built up in the intervening years. "Hey, look. Is that twine?"

Austin moved closer, his head blocking the view. *Dude.* Luke reached up to flick his brother's ear with a finger, but since Blake was with them, changed his mind.

"Yeah." Austin's voice rose an octave. "I think it is. Let me try to get it." He grabbed a stick from the ground to poke at the object in question. Before long, he hooked a loop of a cord and pried a small bag from its hiding place—a slightly larger match to their Sedona find.

"Whoa!" Blake breathed out. "I can't believe it."

Celia let out a little whoop. "Come on, boys. One down, two to go."

They retraced their steps and climbed on the four-wheeler to continue their trek down the trail. Blake did a masterful job of following the narrow path, while Celia kept an eye on the GPS screen to direct the way. Doing this without the cowboy's help would've been nearly impossible. Good thing for Celia's feminine power of persuasion.

"Okay," Celia announced. "This is where the next one should be."

Blake stopped the vehicle, then studied the phone. He glanced down the trail, the dirt path disappearing into the darkness. "The next section is quite steep and narrow. I don't want to risk rolling the four-wheeler, so I think after you retrieve the bag here, you'll need to hike to the third spot."

Austin jumped off the back from their perch. "Let's do it."

Celia slid off her comfortable front seat.

Blake remained seated behind the wheel as he handed Luke the phone. "I think I should probably stay here with the four-wheeler. You never know if we'll run into any hikers or rangers. Wouldn't want them to take the ATV or call it in to the ranger station."

"Makes sense," Austin said. "You be the lookout. Do you know how to whistle to let us know if someone comes?"

Blake emitted a bird call that garnered Austin's approval. "Nice!"

Luke stepped off the trail with Austin trailing behind him, but Celia didn't move. He stopped and looked at her. "Coming?"

She glanced down at her skirt. "You know, I'm not dressed for bushwhacking. I think I'll stay and keep Blake company."

Not dressed appropriately? Good try. She never backed down from a challenge. This was all about spending time alone with her cowboy crush. Whatever. They didn't need her help, anyway. At least, he hoped not. Somehow, four of them searching felt more reassuring than just two.

Replacing doubts or concerns with confidence and determination, Luke shifted into leadership mode. Someone had to take charge. He turned back to the darkness awaiting them. "Okay. Come on, Austin. Let's go."

Chapter 21

Austin:
Player vs. Player

"Come on, Austin. Let's go."

Austin gathered every ounce of courage he could generate as Luke led them into the darkness. He would never admit it to his big brother, but all the trees and rocks with their menacing shapes and angles creeped him out.

He wracked his brain, trying to think of something to say to break the silence. A pun, a witty comment, an interesting fact—anything. But he drew a complete blank. In the silence, weird sounds of nature amplified, increasing his unease. A rustle here, a chirp there, a snap of a branch, an odd whistle. It was enough to make a guy want to whimper. The only thing worse would be if he were alone. Celia had made the right decision staying behind with Blake.

Yes! A topic to discuss. "Celia seems to really like Blake."

Luke pointed the flashlight at the rocks in front of them. "Yeah, I guess."

"She's been so moody for, like, the last year." A rustle in a clump of tall grasses made him edge closer to Luke.

The flashlight beam swept to the other side of the trail. "Ya think?"

Luke's sarcasm didn't cease Austin's chatter that helped calm his nerves. "And I haven't seen her with her old friends in forever. Did she hang out with them at school?"

"She just needs to find herself." The way his brother emphasized the words indicated that the subject was closed.

But Austin ignored the finality of his brother's tone. "By wearing black and never talking to anyone?" He'd seen the way Luke watched Celia, and knew they shared the same concerns. *Why won't he admit it?*

Luke kept moving forward. "Never mind. You wouldn't understand."

Why does he always have to treat me like a little kid? Frustration burned inside him. "Don't be a jerk. What wouldn't I understand?"

"Just forget it." Luke's words snapped louder than any broken branch. "High school is tough for some people. You'll find out *someday.*"

Austin opened his mouth to make the point that Luke wasn't *that* much older, when he spotted the formation. At least, it looked like the one from the photograph. But it was so hard to tell in the dark with all the weird, twisted shadows.

"Hey, isn't that what we're looking for?"

"Nah, we're not there yet." Luke didn't even bother to look where Austin pointed.

Austin was ninety percent sure that the clump of rocks off to the right *was* the one they were searching for. Should he insist they check it out? But what if he made a big deal about it and then was wrong? He could picture Luke's smug look.

Austin dutifully followed a few steps further, then glanced back at the formation. *That's got to be the one.* "Fine. Keep walking, but I'm going to search this spire."

Austin turned and started back to his destination, but without the light, he stumbled over a rock. Luckily, he caught himself before faceplanting in the dirt.

From behind him came an annoyed huff. "Don't be dumb. We need to stick together."

Austin's anger began to boil. *"You* don't be dumb. This is the right one. I know it." *What's his problem?* With everyone else, Luke was so nice and thoughtful, but he treated his own brother like sludge.

The flashlight beam scanned the rock he was heading toward. Austin held his breath, hoping he really was right. An I-told-you-so moment would totally bite.

Luke aimed the light at the rocks. "Fine. That *might* be it."

You're welcome. What's someone got to do to get some respect around here?

"Hold this." Luke shoved the flashlight into Austin's hand as he walked around the back of the spires.

"There's a small opening between the roots and the crevices in the rocks." Austin bent down to get a better look. "Maybe the bag is stuffed in there."

Luke nudged in front of him. "Let me do it. You just hold the light."

"Why don't you think I can do anything?" Austin's composure snapped with anger and frustration. "You always treat me like a little kid." Obviously, not the best time to start an argument, but he'd had it with Luke's attitude.

"Then stop acting like a whiny toddler." Luke shoved his hand into the opening.

Austin watched as Luke grunted and shifted his weight, trying to get his bulky arm into the small space.

"Let me try." Austin grimaced at the slight whine in his voice.

Luke sat back on his heels. "Yeah, I guess this one needs a skinny little kid's arm to reach it."

Biting his lower lip to keep from lashing out, he handed Luke the flashlight, then crouched and slid his hand past dirt, rocks, roots, dead leaves, and something soft that he did not want to even ponder. Finally, his fingers brushed against material. His heart lurched. *Got it!* He pinched his thumb and forefinger around it and tugged. It didn't budge. Decades of debris and mud created a kind of cement.

His legs throbbed from crouching, so he shifted onto his stomach to dig at the encasement around the pouch with his fingernails.

"Any day now." Luke's foot, inches from Austin's face, began tapping.

"How do you have any friends? You're such a jerk sometimes."

Luke started humming the tune from *Jeopardy.*

Amazing that some brothers actually get along.

Finally, Austin dug away enough of the hard earth to pull out the bag.

"Ta da!" He held up the bag in victory.

Luke snatched it out of his hand. "Good. Now let's move. We've been here too long. Mom and Dad are going to start worrying about us."

Austin brushed his grimy hand on his jeans. Shoulda known he'd get no recognition. No "Good job" or "Nice work." Nothin'.

In silence they scrambled down a rocky hill in search of the next spot. Traversing the landscape was no easy task. Loose dirt and rocks made their feet slip down the decline. Once they were on more stable ground, Luke checked the phone to guide their way. Finally, a whitish spire came into view. The light illuminated the arch behind it. The third and final location.

Grandma had told them that the last pouch was hidden in a small cave behind the arch. To keep it secure, she and Harry had rolled a large rock in front of the opening.

"Hold this." Luke shoved Mom's phone into Austin's chest.

Austin pocketed the device while his brother laid the flashlight on the ground to provide some light. Luke pressed his shoulder against the boulder, looking like the football player that he was so proud to be. He shoved, letting out a grunt as he pushed. Nothing happened.

Not surprising. Again, years of rain, snow, and wind had wedged the rock into place. Luke reluctantly let Austin help. They dug around the base, then pushed with all their might. On the third attempt, the heavy rock moved.

We did it! "Well, this is it. I feel like we should say something profound. Like, 'It might be the end of Operation Coin-Find, but the family adventures will continue.'"

"Can you ever just face the task at hand without making a huge deal of everything?" Luke stooped down and pointed the flashlight into the small cave.

Austin crouched down, but his view was blocked by his brother's big head. Luke reached in and tugged at something. His bicep bulged with the exertion. Finally, the object gave way, and Luke fell backward on his butt. Austin clamped his mouth shut to keep from laughing. Luke held up his hand, the third and final bag clutched in his fist.

"Awesome." They'd found all the bags—that was huge! Too bad Celia hadn't come with them so he could have someone to celebrate with. Instead, he was stuck with total-pain Luke.

Luke snatched the flashlight, then stood, brushing off his jeans. "It's getting late. Let's head back before Mom and Dad start searching for us."

Having had enough, Austin held out his hand. "Fine. I'll lead the way. Let me have the flashlight."

Luke smirked. "Funny. Let's move out."

Tired of his brother's arrogance, he lunged for the flashlight.

Luke stepped backwards to avoid Austin's reach. His sneer turned to surprise, then his arms began to flail. The scrambling of the rocks was the only sound that filled the night air. Then Luke dropped out of sight.

Austin stared at the spot where his brother had just been standing. *What . . . ?* The dim moonlight revealed a dark ridge. His insides prickled with sickening understanding.

Luke had just fallen off a cliff into the canyon.

Chapter 22

Celia:
Orange Crush Defense

"You're serious?" Blake's eyebrows rose in disbelief. "You're telling me you've never seen *The Lord of the Rings?*"

They were reclining on the hood of the four-wheeler, enjoying the clear night sky while waiting for the boys to return.

A giggle slipped out. Celia had never been a giggling type of girl, but something about this boy brought them on. "I didn't say I'd *never* seen it. I just don't like it."

He threw his head back. "What? How could you possibly not like it? It's a classic."

"All that fighting. Yuck." She shivered, unsure if the chill came from the thought of those scenes she despised or the cool night air in the canyon.

"You just need someone to explain all the Christian symbolism."

"Funny, I don't remember learning about elves and hobbits in my catechism classes."

He let out a hearty laugh. "You're impossible. Tolkien is probably the most famous Catholic author ever."

"Just for you, I'll consider giving him a second chance." The whole conversation had started when Blake noticed the crucifix necklace around her neck, the one she'd purchased in Santa Fe.

His head rolled her way. "I do have a question for you, my little Catholic friend, although since you're no Tolkien fan, I'm not sure you can help."

"Bring it on. I'll try my best, but if it has something to do with Gandalf, you're on your own." Even though her brothers had been gone longer than expected, she hoped they continued to take their time. She was in no hurry to end her alone time with Blake.

He nudged her with his elbow. "No, I honestly have a question. Someone told me that Catholics worship Mary and the saints. It sounded kinda whack, but what do I know?"

Her eyebrows furrowed as she tried to assess his sincerity. "Are you being serious?"

His hands raised in surrender. "Totally."

He looked earnest, but that was about the dumbest thing she'd ever heard. "Um . . . that makes even less sense than the whole *Lord of the Rings* trilogy."

His eyes flashed. "Hey, now. Stop hatin' on my movie."

She grinned. "Now that I think about it, there is one thing I like about the movie."

"See . . ." He nodded in appreciation.

"Orlando Bloom."

A loud groan accompanied the shake of his head. "Pathetic."

It would be so easy to keep joking, but she felt a niggling to answer his question in case he really was serious. *Please, Lord, give me the right words.* "Back to your question. No, Catholics don't worship Mary or the saints. We respect and honor Mary. I mean, think about it, God chose her, out of all the people that ever lived, to be the mother of our Savior."

His head tilted to the side. "Hmm . . . never really thought of it like that."

"So, we ask Mary and the saints, who are closer to Jesus than we are, to pray for us. Just like you'd ask a friend to pray for you."

Celia was about to say more, but her own words stopped her. Thanks to Grandma's advice, she'd begun praying again, but why hadn't she been asking Jesus' heavenly buddies for help? Her confirmation saint, St. Therese, could surely help a girl out as she unraveled the mess of her life. After all this time, why was this only dawning on her now? Sadly, she'd been so absorbed in feeling sorry for herself that it had never occurred to her.

"Makes sense." Blake brushed a soft curl off his forehead.

Feeling emboldened, she continued, hopefully not killing the mood. "For instance, in the Hail Mary prayer, we say 'Pray for us.' We're not praying *to* her but *with* her." Inspired, she silently vowed that before bed, she'd pray the Rosary.

His serious contemplation shifted into an adorable smirk. "My faith in you is restored. After learning your views on Tolkien, I was seriously questioning your Catholicity."

Her hand flew to her mouth to stifle a laugh. "Catholicity? I'm going to have to use that one."

"Only if you give me credit."

"Deal." She closed her eyes and tried to soak in the perfect moment. "Do you ever wish upon a star?"

"Not in a few years."

She turned to look at him as he watched the stars. "Why can't life be filled with perfect moments such as this?"

He again looked toward her. "Who says it can't?"

"Life." She let out a sigh. "I just dread heading back home." *I barely know this guy. Why is he so easy to confide in?*

"Why?"

She rubbed her bare arms, chilled from the cool night air, then watched the velvety sky in search of a shooting star. "I don't know. This summer has been an amazing adventure. I wish it could continue."

She felt his gaze on her. "Why not make your own adventure. Try something new."

"Maybe." If only it were that easy. But how do you let go of the tormenting hurt and anger from betrayal?

She squeezed her eyes shut. *Please, God, help me find a way to move forward and find those elusive new friends that Grandma claims are out there.*

Maybe there were more good people around than she realized. After all, there was one sitting right next to her. Why was she worried about taking a few risks and stepping out of her comfort zone—which had become way too dark and stifling. What was the worst that could happen? She couldn't sink much lower. She snuck a peek at Blake, his smile aimed at her. A little flutter stirred within her; darn he was cute.

"So, this treasure hunt has been the highlight of your summer?" Blake's question broke the stillness of the night.

"Yeah, and reconnecting with my brothers. What's been the highlight of yours?"

"Meeting you."

She stared at that handsome face, not sure how she was still alive since her heart had just stopped beating. *Stop obsessing, Celia. Don't take it seriously. He's a cute boy who works with tourists. He probably has sweet-talked a ton of girls this summer.* "Yeah, right," she managed to sputter.

He shifted to prop up on his elbow and look at her. "I mean it. You're different—totally cool."

Me? Another giggle bubbled forth.

His eyes narrowed. "Don't laugh; I'm serious."

"My brothers would beg to differ." And everyone else she'd ever met.

"I have a feeling your brothers don't know the real you."

Truer words might never have been spoken. "Hey, thanks for mentioning the dance. It was a lot of fun. I just wish we didn't have to leave so early." She would've gladly danced with him all evening.

"Yeah, it was fun. But I'm not sure you were entirely truthful in claiming you've never line danced. You picked it up rather quickly."

She laughed. "I don't know how you can say that considering the number of times I stomped on your toes."

He shook his head. "You're a great dancer. You should keep it up."

"We'll see." A hint of an idea began to percolate in her mind. "Maybe."

"And when you do, maybe you'll think of me."

The fluttering within her increased in tempo. "Absolutely." This was a memory she would never forget.

Her eyes locked onto his mesmerizing gaze. After a moment, his focus shifted from her eyes to her mouth. *Oh.* She swallowed the lump in her throat.

As he leaned in, she closed her eyes, ready for her first kiss. *Breathe.* But Blake's warm lips didn't find hers. Instead, the gentle kiss landed on her forehead. Her eyes fluttered open to see him watching her with eyes that sparkled in the moonlight. A real kiss might have been phenomenal, but she couldn't be disappointed that her cowboy was a perfect gentleman.

He reached out and brushed one of the loose tendrils of hair from her face. "I wish you weren't leaving tomorrow."

She sighed with the competing emotions of contentment and disappointment. "You and me both." Why can't the amazing people she'd met this summer live in Colorado?

He shifted to drape his arm around her shoulders and pull her close, his body heat immediately warming her. She rested her head against his shoulder as they leaned back to watch the dazzling night sky display once again. *Too bad wishing upon a star can't make this moment last.*

A scrambling off to the right disturbed the beautiful moment. She turned to see Austin rushing toward them.

"Celia! Blake! Something's happened to Luke."

- - - X - - -

She wouldn't exactly describe Austin as the boy who cried wolf, but her younger brother had been known to pull pranks. Needless to say, finding her snuggled next to a guy would be an opportune moment for such a stunt, so she didn't react at first when he charged toward them. But as he neared, the panic on his face became obvious. He was serious.

Before she could react, Blake slid off the hood of the ATV. "What happened?"

Austin held his side as he described Luke's fall, between gasps of breath. Blake asked appropriate questions while Celia sat there gaping. Austin's words swirled around her but never quite penetrated her dazed confusion. Obviously, she was not the person to depend on in a crisis.

Blake grabbed her hand, pulling her back to reality. "You okay?" His concern was the sweetest thing ever.

"Oh. Yeah. Sorry." She slid off the hood hoping her wobbly legs would hold her.

Blake turned back to Austin. "I have a rope here on the ATV. Do you think we can get to him?"

Austin squeezed his eyes shut and shook his head. Even though there were no visible tears, she knew her brother well enough to know that he was trying to shake them away. "I don't think he'll be able to get himself out. It's a sharp cliff, and he's in a lot of pain. He thinks he broke his arm."

Oh man. We are so busted. She jolted back, embarrassed by her thoughts. How could she be more worried about getting in trouble than about Luke? *Sorry, God. Please protect Luke and help him to be all right. Blessed Mother, please be my intercessor, you know better than I what Luke needs right now. Amen.*

"Can you show me on your GPS tracker where he fell?" Blake remained in control, while Celia's hands began to shake uncontrollably. "Maybe there's a road that goes down to that spot." Blake was definitely the go-to guy you wanted around in an emergency—cool, calm, and collected. Not a useless basket case whose mind wandered aimlessly.

Austin pulled Mom's phone from his pocket. The two guys hovered over the screen.

"Hmm." Blake rubbed the back of his neck. "I think I know how to get there, but it's so dark. I worry we could get lost since it's not on the trail."

"Even with the GPS location?" At least Austin's voice had lost its panicky tremble.

"There are some restricted areas and tough terrain that I'm not too familiar with. I think we need help. Let's head back up, and I'll find someone who knows the area better. Besides, if Luke's seriously injured, we'll need help lifting and carrying him."

Austin's forehead creased. "You guys go get help. I don't want to leave him."

Blake turned to look at her. "Okay. Austin will stay here. Celia, you come with me." He lifted the passenger seat of the ATV to reveal a storage compartment. He removed a rope and a bottle of water and handed both to Austin.

Feeling lightheaded, she leaned against the vehicle while the boys coordinated their plan. A moment later, Austin slipped back into the darkness.

Blake took her hands. His warmth brought her back into focus. "Don't worry. Everything's going to be okay."

She nodded, then slid into the vehicle.

Blake walked around the ATV and settled into the driver's seat, then turned to her. "I'm serious. Luke will be fine." His hand grasped hers. "He just has the worst timing ever."

She turned to look at him. His wink made her feel slightly better. She couldn't keep from smiling, despite the circumstances. *So true.* The first time in forever that she had felt happy and normal, and the moment was gone in an instant.

As they drove up the trail, a realization burst through her bubble of regret. She was truly thankful for meeting Blake because even though their time together was brief, it seemed to spark something within her.

- - - X - - -

The best-case scenario would be if they could quickly locate Blake's coworkers or uncle, then slip back down into the canyon without anyone noticing. But luck was not on Celia's side. As soon as they neared the barn, she spotted her parents and grandmother outside talking to Cowboy Mel.

Dad's eyes narrowed as he watched Blake and Celia pull up. Celia could practically see the steam spurting from his ears as he stormed toward them. *Yikes. This will not go smoothly.*

"Dad," she began, but he didn't let her continue.

"I thought you were with your brothers." His raised voice drew unwanted attention toward them. "Were they covering for you so you could sneak off with some guy?"

"Dad . . ." She tried again, forcing her gaze away from the bulging vein in his neck. "It's not what you think."

"So, you haven't been alone with a strange boy when you should have been at this dance?"

Why is he going so ballistic? She glanced at Mom, searching for a glimmer of support but found none.

"Sir, can we explain?" Blake was one brave guy.

Dad jabbed his finger toward Blake. "No! You may not explain anything!"

The crowd of spectators grew. So much for quietly sneaking in.

"Dad!"

"Don't you raise your voice. Get away from this punk and go back to the campground." His venomous tone made her want to run and hide, but instead, she squared her shoulders and forced herself to stand strong.

"Would you please listen? Luke is injured!"

That news stopped Pit Bull Dad. His face transformed from anger to confusion.

Mom rushed forward and grabbed Celia's hands. "What happened?"

Finally. She took a deep breath. "The four of us were down in the canyon, and Luke fell. We think maybe he broke his arm."

"We came to get help so we can reach him." Blake didn't hang around for Dad's response but quickly made his way toward the barn.

"Where's Austin?" Mom gripped Celia's hand even tighter.

"He stayed down there. He didn't want Luke to wait by himself."

Dad recovered from his initial shock. Now that he knew she wasn't completely alone with a cute boy, his anger subsided. "What on earth were you doing on the trails in the dark?"

Her gaze shifted toward Grandma. "We were just . . . checking things out."

"What things?" Dad demanded.

"Oh dear." Grandma clutched Dad's arm. "I think this is my fault."

Dad looked between his daughter and his mother. "What are you talking about?"

Blake and two other men strode out of the barn.

Whew. Perfect timing.

"Dad, we'll explain later. We need to get back to the boys."

Mom wrapped an arm around her mother-in-law. "What can we do?"

Celia embraced them. "Pray."

Grandma

Harry,

My hand is shaking so much, making it hard to write. I'm not sure I'll even send this, but I just have to write something down. The kids went searching for the bags in the dark, and now Luke is hurt. I don't know yet how extensive his injuries are. I'm scared for him and so full of guilt for keeping this adventure a secret from their parents. What was I thinking? My prayers are the only way to help him now.

Grace

Chapter 23

LUKE:
DOWN FOR THE COUNT

Please, Lord. Please, Lord. This monotonous mantra was all that Luke could come up with. He'd been trying to recite some prayers, but the pain was so intense, he couldn't focus—not even long enough to recite The Lord's Prayer or a Hail Mary. He'd been banged up before, but nothing had ever hurt this bad.

The less critical pain came from rocks jutting into his back and hip, but every time he tried to move, the torture from his injured arm pierced his entire body with an intensity so sharp he was afraid of losing consciousness.

Please, Lord. Please help me. Please send help. Possibly the worst part was knowing he was relying on Austin for some kind of rescue. *Some help that is.* The realization that it could take hours for help to arrive filled him with a despair that he hadn't even known existed.

Austin. Why had he insisted on grabbing the stupid flashlight? He was most likely lost in the canyon somewhere. *I should've just gone by myself to search for the bags. We'd be back at the dance by now.*

The penetrating stab of the rock jabbing his side felt like it was puncturing a vital organ. He slowly shifted to relieve the pressure. *OW!* White spots clouded his vision. He bit his lip until the bitter taste of blood turned his stomach. He focused on taking short breaths until the pain became bearable once again.

No doubt about it. His arm was busted. *So much for my football season.* All because Austin felt like he had something to prove.

Luke squeezed his eyes shut. Now what? His life seemed to be unraveling before his eyes. Gone were his girlfriend and football season. Undoubtably losing both would affect his standing in their friend group. His whole high school identity had been dismantled as he'd hit rock bottom—literally. He opened his eyes; thousands of stars came into focus. Maybe it was time to follow Grandma's advice and trust in God.

Okay, God. You got my attention. My plans certainly haven't been working out, so let's see the path You want me to take. Since it's out of my hands, I'm giving it all to You.

"Luke!" Austin's voice wafted down from the ledge above.

"Yeah." Luke could hear the raspy strain in his own voice.

"You okay?"

Am I okay? What do you think? He gritted his teeth. "No."

"Um . . . okay."

Here it comes. His little brother has come back to admit that he's lost. He can't find Celia. No help is on the way. Luke closed his eyes and waited through another wave of pain. As he focused once again on breathing, he realized Austin continued to talk. The kid had always been a nervous talker, but this rambling montage was not his usual evenly paced diatribe. It was broken up with grunts and heavy breaths.

"Okay, coming down."

What? No! Find help. It took Luke a moment to realize that he hadn't actually spoken the thoughts—the pain made it too difficult.

"No," he managed to utter.

Something dropped off the cliff, landing nearby. Unable to turn his head, Luke noticed a dark shape sliding down the cliff out of the corner of his eye. Too late. Austin was coming down. Desperation washed over him. What an idiotic move. How were they going to get help now? The kid dropped to the ground, squatting next to him. The concerned gaze infuriated Luke.

This is your fault.

"Oh man. You look horrible."

Luke squeezed his eyes shut, fighting through another burst of pain. "We. Need. Help."

"Don't worry. I've got it covered. Blake and Celia are on their way back to the lodge."

He'd done it? The kid had somehow found them? *Thank you, Lord.*

Austin continued rambling. "The problem is I don't know how long it will take them to find help and get a rescue team organized." He pulled out a flashlight. Luke squinted as the beam shone in his eyes. "You look like you're in pretty bad shape. Your arm . . ." Austin's eyes widened. "Um . . . doesn't look quite right. Is that the most painful injury?"

Luke managed to nod.

"Okay." Austin glanced around, then scrambled out of sight.

The sounds of him shuffling around were surprisingly comforting. Amazing how reassuring it was to have someone else nearby—to not be alone in this mess—even if it was only his kid brother.

Austin bent down next to him again. "Okay. I'm going to splint your arm."

Luke's eyes flew open. "No," he managed to mutter through clenched teeth. The thought of his arm being moved made him want to hurl.

Austin leaned closer. "Trust me. Every time you move, the pain in your arm is probably excruciating. You're lying on sharp rocks, and who knows how long it'll take for help to come. We've gotta get you a little more comfortable. I won't bend your arm or anything. Promise. But if we immobilize it and stop the bones from shifting, it'll feel a little better."

Austin must've taken Luke's grimace as a sign of approval, because without any further discussion, he held up a small stick. "I want you to bite on this while I work."

Luke managed to shoot him a warning look, but Austin just shook his head. "It helped Civil War soldiers make it through amputations. It will work."

Not convinced the twisted logic made sense, Luke reluctantly opened his mouth and let Austin slide the stick between his teeth.

"Great." Then the kid held up a longer, sturdier branch and his belt. "Now, I'm going to stabilize your arm. It'll probably be pretty painful for a moment, but then it will feel better."

Luke sank his teeth into the stick. The last thing he saw before squeezing his eyes shut was Austin making the sign of the cross.

Please, Lord. Please, Lord.

An excruciating pain jolted through every cell of his body.

"Sorry." Austin's voice sounded far away and muffled. Luke attempted to open his eyes, but everything turned black.

- - - X - - -

"Luke. *Luke.*" Austin's soft, yet urgent voice penetrated the void.

Luke's eyes didn't want to cooperate, but he finally forced them open.

Austin's concerned face peered down at him. "You all right?"

Luke glanced around. *Where am I?*

His brother's hand pushed down on his chest, keeping him from sitting up. "Hold on. Don't move. You fell, remember?"

The hunt for the treasure. The cliff. His arm. He grimaced.

Austin released a deep breath, then sank down to sit next to him. "Dang. You scared me. I think you passed out." The back of his fist rubbed his eye. *Is he crying?* "I was trying to help. Didn't mean to hurt you."

Suddenly, the rock stabbing the middle of his back was the only thing Luke could think about. All he wanted to do was shift his weight, but the memory of the crushing pain kept him from moving.

Austin brushed away one more tear, then leaned close once again. "Okay. Let's see if we can move you a little. Maybe if I roll you, I can get the larger rocks out from under you."

Luke held his breath, ready to give it a try.

"Don't try to move your arm," Austin commanded. "Keep it tight against your chest. I don't want to touch your shoulder; it's too close to your injury. Instead, I'm going to push your hip up slowly."

Austin offered the small stick once again. *Must have fallen out of my mouth when I passed out.* Luke again clenched down on the wood as Austin pushed Luke's right hip toward the sky. A jolt of pain zapped down his arm, but it wasn't quite as bone-crushing as before.

His brother slowly lowered him. Ah . . . finally, no sharp rocks.

Austin held up a bottle of water. Nothing had ever sounded better. Luke eagerly accepted Austin's assistance to lift his head for a drink.

"Thanks, man." Being so vulnerable was the worst.

Austin offered a strained smile. "Hey. I'm really sorry I caused you to fall."

Luke squelched the temptation to agree, knowing that wouldn't be fair. He took a deep breath. "Wasn't all your fault. I was being a jerk. You didn't seem to be taking the whole wandering-around-a-canyon-in-the-dark thing seriously, so I felt like I needed to take charge. Guess I let the stress get to me."

Austin bit his lower lip, then looked off to the left. "Sometimes you act like I'm still a little kid, and it really gets annoying."

Luke thought back to the last few minutes, and how his brother had totally taken charge of the situation. Austin was right. Luke often treated him as a little kid, but apparently, that wasn't completely fitting anymore. Somewhere along the way, Austin had started to mature. "Yeah, I guess I have trouble thinking of you as anything other than that. Sorry."

Austin's face scrunched up. "Okay."

"Hey, the splint was a good idea." It was unbelievable how much it helped control the pain.

Relief relaxed his brother's strained face. "Good."

"How'd you know what to do?"

A goofy grin crossed Austin's face. "One of the soldiers in my video game did something similar to help a wounded comrade."

A small laugh escaped. *Figures.* "Wow. Guess I can't razz you for playing your games anymore."

The grin shifted into a smirk. "You know, I haven't missed them too much the last few days."

"How long you think it'll take for help to arrive?" Hopefully, not long.

Austin peered toward the top of the cliff. "I keep picturing Celia and Blake showing up at the barn alone. So, the better question is, how long do you think it will take Celia to convince Dad that she didn't sneak off with the guy and that we are actually in trouble?"

Despite the pain, Luke couldn't help but grin, picturing Dad's reaction to that. And he thought *he* was in a tough situation. "You're right. It might be a while. Poor Celia."

Chapter 24

Austin:
End Game

Why didn't I ever learn to read lips? Austin watched Dad speak to the head ranger, scrutinizing every movement. He had no idea what was being said, but the worry lines on Dad's face seemed to deepen by the minute. Not a good sign. Dad's eyes kept darting toward Mom, who hadn't left Luke's side since he'd been rescued. Luke's weird gray coloring gave him the appearance of a zombie from one of Austin's games. *Why did this have to happen? Why didn't I just let Luke have his way?* His stomach churned with worry and guilt. *Please, God, let Luke be okay.*

Austin, Grandma, and Celia sat in the lodge, helplessly awaiting further instruction. They remained huddled together in a comfy sitting area by the massive lodge fireplace. Blake and a few other employees who had helped with Luke's rescue hovered off to the side. Blake and Celia bravely exchanged quick glances. Hopefully, for their sake, Dad didn't notice.

Through the evening's ordeal, Austin had lost all track of time. It must be late since all the other guests at the resort seemed to have gone to bed. He clenched his hands. At least they were back at the lodge. Waiting in that desolate canyon for help to arrive had felt like an eternity. Then when the cavalry had finally shown up, the park rangers' debating about whether or not to call in an ambulance and rescue personnel had taken forever. In the end, they'd decided Luke's only serious injury was his arm. The consensus had been that he was stable enough for them to get him out of the canyon faster than if they waited for a rescue crew. They'd had some equipment to stabilize his arm further but seemed impressed with the impromptu splint. Hopefully, it had helped.

Dad eventually shook hands with the official, then watched as they wheeled Luke out to the ambulance that had finally arrived. After saying a few words to Mom before she joined Luke, he turned and walked toward his waiting family. *What do those creases in his face mean? Is he worried? Angry? About to disown us?*

Grandma stood as Dad neared. "What did they say? Should we go with you to the hospital?"

Dad shook his head. "There's no need for everyone to go. You three stay here. The hospital is about a half-hour away, and the ranger has offered to drive me down. I have no idea how long we'll be, but we'll worry about getting back here later." His gaze quickly shifted to Celia and Austin. "You all head back to the motorhome and get some sleep."

Austin longed to say something. Anything. But Dad's on-edge, about-to-lose-it look made him swallow any possible words. *Besides, what is there to say? It's all my fault.*

"We'll keep him in our prayers." Grandma squeezed Dad's arm.

Dad's head tilted, then his eyes narrowed in on Austin. *Oh, no.* "Luke tells me that you helped a lot by making that splint. Good job."

Austin bit the inside of his cheek, not wanting the praise. "If I hadn't been arguing with him, he wouldn't have fallen, and he wouldn't have needed the dumb splint. And now he won't be able to play football this year." Just saying the words brought tears to his eyes.

Dad grimaced.

Grandma sank back into the chair she had been occupying. "There's enough blame to go around. If it wasn't for me, none of you would have been down in the canyon."

Dad lowered down into a squat, eye-level with everyone. "Listen, I have to go, but we will be having a family talk tomorrow." His eyes travelled slowly between the three of them. "I have no idea what is going on between you all, but you have some explaining to do."

Austin glanced at Celia, who returned his gaze. They nodded in unison. *Fair enough.*

Grandma cleared her throat. "That's probably a good idea."

Dad rose, then hurried out the door to the ranger vehicle waiting to transport him to the hospital.

The remaining employees began to exit as well. Guess they realized there was nothing more to see. With Dad gone, Celia made her way over to Blake.

"Those two seem to be hitting it off," Grandma said.

Austin leaned back in the chair, letting his head fall against the cushion. "Yeah, looks that way." Suddenly, exhaustion swept over him. "Well, tonight sure didn't go as planned."

"That is an understatement if I ever heard one." Grandma let out a deep sigh. "Why did you decide to look for the treasure tonight? I thought the plan was to go hiking tomorrow?"

He rolled his head, turning his face toward her. "We figured there would be more people on the trails tomorrow, increasing the difficulty of a search. We didn't know if we'd get in trouble hiking off-trail. When Celia suggested asking for Blake's help, well, it seemed like a good idea at the time." *If only they'd kept to the original plan.* "I guess the good news is we found the bags."

Grandma closed her eyes for a moment, then reached over to pat his hand. "Austin, don't blame yourself for Luke's injury. I feel guilty, too, but it doesn't do any good to dwell on what might have been. All we can do is figure out what we can learn from the situation, then move on."

Unsure if he could answer without crying, he replied with a shrug, even though he didn't completely agree.

"Do you want to talk about your argument with Luke?" Grandma's soft voice offered some comfort.

"I was just so frustrated with him because he was treating me like a little kid—again." He took a deep breath. "Guess I proved him right." Why couldn't he have controlled his temper?

Grandma squeezed his hand. "Sounds like your quick thinking really helped. Creating a splint doesn't sound like something a little kid would do."

He shook his head. He knew she was trying to make him feel better, but it wasn't working.

She leaned closer. "Sometimes those who know us the best are the ones who know us the least."

His eyes narrowed. "Huh?"

"Just like it took my daddy a while to see the man Charlie became, it might take your siblings a little time to see you as someone other than their little brother. Just keep being yourself, and sooner or later, they will see the amazing young man you are becoming."

"Thanks." Austin offered a little smile, unconvinced that would ever happen, because he'd forever be nothing but Luke and Celia's little brother.

From behind Grandma, Celia and Blake approached, their hands hidden behind their backs. The mischievous smiles completely out of place.

Noticing Austin's gaze, Grandma turned to watch them. "What are you two up to?"

Celia's eyebrows wiggled. "We thought the hero among us should be rewarded."

Austin sat up a little straighter. "Who are you talking about?"

"You!" Celia's hands emerged from behind her back, an ice cream cone in each of them.

He stared at the cone she offered him, grateful for the thoughtful gesture.

Blake revealed two cones as well. He handed one to Grandma, then sat next to Celia to enjoy the dessert.

Austin licked the cold treat. "Thanks, but I don't know why I'm the hero."

Celia's eyes widened. "Are you kidding? Even the emergency-trained rangers were impressed with that splint you made."

Blake nodded his agreement. "How'd you think to do that?"

His shoulders rose in a shrug. "I don't know. It just seemed like the thing to do." He didn't mention the video game aspect. That could be his and Luke's little secret.

"Well, it was impressive." Celia delicately touched her tongue to her cone. Probably didn't want to give it her usual whole-hearted lick in front of Blake. Sheesh.

Grandma wiped the corner of her mouth with the napkin that had been wrapped around the cone. "Austin, you are the one to have around in an emergency."

"Much better than me," Celia said. "I totally froze, right?" She looked at Blake.

Blake shook his head. "You were fine."

Maybe it was the cold treat, or possibly the nice words, but something caused Austin to feel slightly better. "Besides, Celia, you had the hard part of telling Dad."

Celia exchanged a look with Blake. "Yeah, that was not pretty."

Blake shared a smile with her. "See? You're braver than you think you are."

They all chatted for a few more minutes as they finished their cones, but soon, each one was stifling yawns.

"I'll drive you all back to your campsite on the ATV," Blake offered.

Grandma covered her yawn with her hand. "That would be very kind. Thank you."

Austin shook his head. *Nice move, cowboy.* He would bet money that Blake's gentlemanly offer had less to do with making sure they didn't have to walk all the way back to the campground in the middle of the night and more to do with spending a few more minutes with Celia. No complaints, though. He much preferred the happy, infatuated Celia to the sullen, cranky one they'd been living with for the past year.

Grandma

Dear Diary,

As we travel down the road, rolling along to our next destination, I keep thinking about the coins we left behind in Bryce. Someday, someone might find them. I keep wondering who it might be. Next week, one of the cowboys leading a family into the canyon could notice the little cloth bundles that shouldn't be there. Or ten years from now, a tourist taking photos of the spires could see something that doesn't belong. In twenty years, a park ranger leading a tour through the canyon could discover one of them. Or maybe right now a bird is trying to untie the bags to use the twine for her nest. The possibilities are exciting to think about.

Oh! In other news, I finally know what I want to be when I grow up. A travel writer. I didn't even know it was a thing, but Harry showed me some of his National Geographic magazines. He said people actually get paid to travel all over the world and write about it. Can you believe that? Good thing Mama got me this journal so I can practice my writing. Maybe that's my talent. Although, I'm not so great with a camera so, I'll need someone else to take all the photos. Hey! Maybe that future best friend/husband of mine can do the job. That would solve everything.

Hasta la vista! (Daddy says that means, "see ya later" in Spanish. I figure it's never too early to start learning a few phrases for when I begin traveling the world.)

Gracie

Chapter 25

Celia:
Following the Yellow Brick Road

A wet lick sliding across her cheek pulled Celia from a dream. Not an ideal way to wake up, albeit effective. Her eyes squinted open and peered straight into Siena's big brown ones. Happy to have accomplished her wake-up call, Siena rolled onto her back, ready for a tummy rub. So needy.

As Celia acquiesced to Siena's demand, her mind drifted to the previous night. Luke's injury. Dad's fury. Blake's gorgeous eyes. Her insides turned to mush with that memory. But then reality hit, causing her heart to sink. They were scheduled to leave today, and she would most likely never see her handsome cowboy again.

After he had driven them back from the lodge and they'd said goodnight to Grandma and Austin, she and Blake had chatted late into the night. They'd exchanged numbers, but she knew keeping in touch would be futile. It wasn't like they could easily get together. She'd just have to treasure the time they'd spent together. *Does one evening count as a summer romance?*

"Hey." Austin pushed himself to a sitting position. A chunk of his wild shock of disheveled morning hair fell across one eye. "Think Luke's still at the hospital?"

She glanced toward the empty sleeping bag. "I'm not sure."

"I hope he's feeling better." Her little brother muttered through a yawn. "I still feel horrible."

She attempted her most reassuring smile. "I know, but I'm not sure you want to keep telling Luke that. He might take advantage and use your guilt to make you do everything for him."

He let out a little chuckle. "That does sound like something he'd do."

"Believe me, I speak from experience. Why do you think I carried his backpack for him all those months when we were in elementary school?"

His eyes widened. *"What?* Really? I never thought about it. What did you feel guilty about?"

"I'd left his scooter out during a rainstorm, and it rusted."

"Classic." He took in a deep breath. "Smell that?"

She closed her eyes, savoring the delicious, smoky campfire scent that wafted into the tent. "Well, someone's up. Shall we see who's here?"

Austin answered with a groan.

"Come on, time to face the music." She wiggled out of her sleeping bag.

They emerged from the tent to see Grandma sitting in front of a small fire, reading her Bible. She looked up and smiled. "Good morning."

"Morning." Celia curled up on one of the chairs.

"Well, you two certainly slept in." Grandma's gaze locked onto Celia. "You must've been tired after such a late night."

There was no fooling Grandma. Celia and Blake had tried to be quiet but hadn't been able to stop themselves from laughing about one thing or another. "Sorry if we kept you awake."

"I couldn't sleep, anyway. I had a lot to pray about."

Austin plopped down in the chair next to Celia. "How's Luke? Have you heard anything?"

Grandma closed her Bible. "Yes, your dad called a little while ago. Luke will be fine. The break was pretty bad though, so they'd had to operate."

Austin sank further into his chair.

"Your parents stayed overnight at the hospital. But the good news is that Luke's being released this morning, and they should be back in a little while. Mel is giving them a ride."

Surgery. That definitely meant no football. *Poor Luke. He'll be devasted.* Guess he'll be trying something new this year as well.

"Listen," Grandma continued, "I know you both feel bad. I do, as well. But feeling guilty doesn't help anything. What happened was an accident."

She was right, but it didn't stop the possible different outcomes from swirling through Celia's head. What if she had gone with the boys instead of staying with Blake? She could've been the peacekeeper and stopped their argument. Maybe she shouldn't have asked for Blake's help in the first place. Then they would be down in the canyon searching at this very moment, instead of waiting for Luke to return from the hospital.

After a mostly silent breakfast, Grandma continued her daily reading while Celia and Austin got ready for the day. The dread of fessing up to Mom and Dad grew with each passing minute. By mid-morning, Celia was a complete bundle of nerves, so when Grandma and Austin decided to take Siena on a walk, she reached for Grandma's Bible and settled into a chair. Ephesians, chapters 4 and 5, were the verses Grandma had told them to read. Celia flipped through the worn Bible to locate them. The passages were easy to find since Grandma had stuck one of her postcards in the Bible to mark them. The first read-through didn't help much since her mind kept drifting to Luke or Blake. The only things she remembered were the verses about husbands and wives. That couldn't be what Grandma wanted them to focus on. She rolled her shoulders and tried again.

- - - X - - -

Celia closed the Bible and set it aside when Grandma and Austin returned. The verses were interesting but hadn't produced the desired effect of calming her nerves. By the time Mel's ginormous truck pulled up next to the RV, Celia's insides were once again on the verge of percolating.

As the group emerged from the truck, she took a quick visual inventory. They certainly were not a very photogenic bunch at the moment. Mom's appearance could only be described as rough, with smeared mascara and visible bags under her eyes. Although, the blonde hair matted to the right side of her head probably indicated that she'd at least gotten a little sleep. Dad was equally ragged, with bloodshot eyes and uncharacteristic stubble. His western shirt, so crisp and clean last night, now was a wrinkled mess. Luke looked exhausted, the way he did after a grueling football practice, but at least he'd lost the unnatural shade of gray that had freaked her out last night. Her gaze quickly traveled to his arm, which now sported a blue cast, one of their school colors.

After thank yous, nice meeting yous, and good lucks, they bid farewell to Cowboy Mel. Too bad he couldn't stay awhile longer and help postpone the looming family meeting.

After Mel drove away, heavy silence settled over the campsite. Grandma insisted on making coffee for the adults before they all talked. While she and Mom took care of that chore, Dad stoked the fizzling fire.

"You okay?" Celia quietly asked Luke as he settled into a chair.

He set his cast on the fabric arm of the chair. "Yeah."

Siena whimpered and inched closer to him, placing her head on his lap—her sixth sense kicking in. She'd always had an uncanny ability to know when someone didn't feel well. Luke's gaze shifted to Austin, who had been warily watching every move he made. "Hey, Austin, the doctors said things could've been worse if you hadn't immobilized my arm. The shattered bone might have done more damage. Good job."

Austin squirmed before answering. "Just thought it might help."

Celia hoped that someday Austin would stop feeling responsible for the fall.

The three of them sat in awkward silence, staring at the fire Dad had successfully brought back to life, until Mom and Grandma emerged from the motorhome with mugs of coffee. Mom handed one to Dad, and the adults all settled around the fire.

Dad took a swig from his mug, then released a long sigh—the signal that their little pow-wow was about to convene. "I would really love an explanation about what happened last night."

When no one jumped in with an explanation, he continued. "I can't figure out why you boys felt the need to go hiking in the canyon after dark, and why you left your sister alone with some random guy, and what irresponsible thing you lured your poor grandmother into?"

"That's not *exactly* what happened." Austin's voice was barely audible above the crackle of the fire.

"Well, then, please fill us in on what exactly happened." Dad's voice dripped with equal parts anger and sarcasm.

Oh gee.

"There is no need for that tone of voice, son," Grandma scolded. "I told you last night that this was my fault, and I meant it. I asked the children to go down into the canyon for me."

Dad rubbed his stubbly jaw. "That's not an explanation."

Mom laid a hand on Dad's arm, then looked at Grandma. "Why would you want them to go into the canyon at night?"

Austin flipped the hair out of his eyes. "She didn't. Grandma thought we would hike down today, but we changed the plan."

"We figured the trail would be less crowded at night, when most people were at the dance," Luke added.

Austin's head bobbed in agreement. "We knew it would be hard to find our way in the dark, so Celia suggested we ask Blake to help us since he knows the trail."

Celia's heart ricocheted around her chest at the mere mention of Blake's name.

Mom's and Dad's faces reflected the fact that this new information did nothing to clear up the situation.

"Okay." Mom heaved a weary sigh and rubbed her temple. "But none of that tells us why Grandma asked you to go down there in the first place."

Celia glanced at Grandma. This was not their secret to share.

Grandma's grip tightened on her mug. "It's a long story."

Dad leaned back and raised his mug. "Well, we're all ears."

Grandma straightened her shoulders. "You see, it started sixty-some years ago."

The uncharacteristic laugh that escaped Dad's lips was completely unexpected. *Who knew he could pull off "snarky teen" so well?*

Mom kicked his shin. "Go on, Grace."

Grandma sent a scolding look Dad's way, then wrapped both hands around her mug. "As I was saying, this began years ago when Harry and I were on our Southwest trip. We were playing some sort of treasure hunt game while our parents were busy working. A man my father was meeting noticed our playacting and handed us a bag of coins and trinkets. He said he thought we needed an actual treasure to hide. We hid some at our campsite in Sedona and more here at Bryce. When I was visiting Harry a few months back, we were reminiscing about the trip and got to wondering if the bags might still be hidden."

Dad leaned forward, interest overpowering his annoyance. "Really?" His gaze fell on each of his children. "You were searching for these bags?"

They nodded in unison—a trio of bobbleheads.

"Well, don't keep us in suspense." Dad turned to look at Mom, then back at them. His eyebrows raised in curiosity. "Did you find them?"

Celia couldn't control her grin, excited to share the news. "Yeah, all four bags."

Dad closed his eyes, then looked toward Grandma. "Why didn't you tell us about this?"

Grandma batted her hand at him. "You are like your father and far too practical. I figured you wouldn't agree to indulge my curiosity by digging for my child-hood treasure."

Dad's mouth opened to protest, then immediately shut as the tension eased from his face.

Mom's fingers tapped her mug. "So, is that why you were out wandering around that night in Sedona?"

Grandma gave a firm, definitive nod. "Yes. But then I realized I couldn't find the bags by myself, so I asked the children to help."

"Wow." Dad ran a hand through his already disheveled hair, causing it to stand on end.

Grandma's sad eyes turned to Luke. "I certainly didn't want anyone to get injured though."

Luke placed his good hand on Grandma's thin shoulder. "It's okay. It was our dumb idea to go searching in the dark."

The family sat in silence, each lost in their own thoughts.

Well, that went smoother than expected. And thank goodness they'd veered away from any more interrogation regarding Blake.

Mom finally broke the prolonged stillness. "Well, I certainly wasn't expecting that. But tell me, are there any more hidden bags of treasure we have to worry about you running off and searching for?"

"No. That part of the adventure is over." Grandma lifted her mug to sip her coffee.

Mom and Dad exchanged a look of relief, but all Celia felt was a sinking feeling of overwhelming disappointment.

Chapter 26

LUKE:
RALLY TIME

Dad once again opened his mouth, presumably to say something, then shut it. After the third try, he finally must have collected his thoughts. "Well, I guess that explains everything. Let's go ahead and break camp. We can probably make it home in two days."

Wait. What? Now it was Luke's turn to have his mouth drop open.

Celia and Grandma's eyes widened, apparently also shocked by this pronouncement.

"Home?" Austin's face scrunched in confusion. "What about Lake Powell?"

Celia's head bobbed in agreement. "Yeah."

Dad's face hardened. "Luke broke his arm. He had to have surgery. The vacation is over. We need to head home."

"What?"

"No."

"Why?"

Their reactions piled out on top of each other.

Luke continued talking before Dad had the chance to answer the collective complaints. "Oh, come on. I'm fine. I have pain meds. What good would it do to go home?" The moment they returned home, he'd have to man up and talk to both Coach and Jenna. Two conversations he would prefer to avoid for a little while longer.

"We're having fun. Don't make us head home," Celia pleaded.

"We still have so much to see!" Austin reacted as if Dad had lost his mind.

Dad turned toward Mom, who shrugged and patted his arm. "You know how I feel. I think we should finish out the trip."

"Please, Dad?" Celia clasped her hands in front of her.

Austin perched on the edge of his chair. "You were so excited about seeing Lake Powell. We can't skip that part of the trip."

Dad's eyes narrowed. "I wasn't expecting this reaction, considering that not one of you wanted to take this trip in the first place."

Austin shrugged. "It's more fun than we thought it would be."

"This is so much better than being back at home." Celia flashed her puppy dog eyes.

Luke lifted his cast. "My football season is shot. There's no reason to hurry back now." The desire to stay overpowered the ache in his arm.

That stopped the pleading. The whole family turned to look at Luke, probably as surprised as he was with the nonchalance of the acknowledgment. Did he really not care about missing the season? Not especially. *Huh. Well, that's a surprise.*

Luke glanced at Grandma, who was taking it all in without a word. This trip had been her dream, and it had nearly slipped away.

Dad raised his hands in surrender. "Fine. We can keep to our schedule."

The corners of Grandma's mouth curled into a slight grin.

"But," Dad continued, "that still means it's time to break camp so we can get on the road."

As the rest of the family moved, Grandma stepped close to Luke. "Luke, I know you might be upset that your injury will keep you from playing football, but instead of dwelling on the disappointment, maybe you can look at the situation in a different light. God can use our setbacks to move us in a new direction and draw us closer to Him." She squeezed his good shoulder, then walked toward the RV, leaving him to think about her words of wisdom.

Closer to God. Had he actually drifted from Him? Of course, he had. His desire to be part of one particular friend group had outweighed everything else. It wasn't like his friends were bad, but they definitely weren't into any kind of faith. Since other church friends had stopped going to youth group, it hadn't seemed like that big a deal. But something about this trip made him feel closer to God than he had in a really long time. And strangely, he didn't have a burning desire to get back in the groove with his friend group. Putting down the phones had been freeing and surprisingly revealing. And now, with him unable to play football, he could easily make a change. A clean break, so to speak.

He looked down at his cast and shook his head. Darn it, Austin. The kid's dumb sense of humor was wearing off on him.

- - - X - - -

He had to admit it—having a broken arm had its perks. No one expected him to help break down the campsite. Maybe he could milk this injury for a little while longer. Though, as fun as it was to watch Austin and Celia struggle with the tent, he wanted to hit the road sometime this century, so offered his tent deconstruction expertise from his supervisor perch at the picnic table.

Celia promptly ignored his advice. "Enjoy your convalescence, big bro. Just remember, if you're feeling well enough to boat and jet ski at Lake Powell, then you're capable of doing your chores."

Austin looked toward him, his eyes squinting. "Are you trying to get out of helping?"

Luke shook his head. "Nah. Never."

Celia's eyes rolled. "Told you, Austin. You have to watch out for The Master of Guilt Trips."

"The Master of Guilt Trips? What would that make you? The Goddess of Moodiness?" Luke quipped back.

She shoved the tent poles into the bag. "I'm not moody."

"Well, I do have to admit that name doesn't exactly apply to you lately."

She smirked and shook her head. "I don't know what you're talking about."

"Seriously, it's been nice seeing you happy." He still had no idea what had been going on with her at school, but maybe this trip was helping her work through it.

"Happy because of *Bla-ake,*" Austin singsonged.

Celia half-heartedly threw one of the pillows at their younger brother. "You're ridiculous. Blake has nothing to do with this conversation."

"Good, then maybe this new, improved, happy Celia will make an appearance at school this year." The moment the words left Luke's mouth, regret washed through him. *Way to ruin the moment.*

His sister's face instantly hardened, and her eyes narrowed. Austin shot him a look. *He's right. I went too far.*

"Sorry, I didn't mean anything by it." Hopefully, she'd accept the apology and move on.

Celia looked away and continued working on the tent. Luke truly intended to change the subject but then suddenly seemed incapable of following the path of least resistance. Maybe it was the pain meds. Maybe it was the exhaustion of always being worried about offending her. Whatever the reason, he boldly—or stupidly—continued. What did he have to lose?

"Celia, I really am sorry if I made you angry. I didn't mean to."

Austin stared at him with bulging eyes, urging him to shut up. He ignored the silent message. "I don't mean to be critical, but I was worried about you last year. Once you got to high school, you became a different person, closing yourself off from everyone, distancing yourself from friends, acting like you hated the world. Then you started hanging out with the fringe." He ignored the daggers shooting from her eyes. "The last few weeks, you've been like the Celia we know and love. I prefer this Celia and hope the other one doesn't come back to Colorado with us." There, he'd said it. No going back now.

She fumed for a moment, then threw the tent pieces on the ground and stormed off.

Well, that didn't go well. He glanced at Austin with a shrug.

Austin shook his head. "Real smooth, bro." He turned back to the task at hand and the pieces of the tent surrounding him, then he glared in disgust. "Now I have to do this all by myself. Thanks a lot."

Chapter 27

Austin:
Good to Go

On the road once again. Austin watched the miles roll past in excruciating silence, except for the mellow Christian tunes Mom had chosen for road-trip music. Mom and Dad once again occupied their usual seats up front, with Siena in her happy spot—perched between them watching the road ahead. Curled up in a chair, Celia worked on a sketch. Luke played a game of aptly named Solitaire. Austin didn't even have Grandma to talk to. She was in the back, resting or something. Oh, what he wouldn't give to have his phone again!

Sprawled across the bench behind the table, he stared out the window and watched the scenery whiz past. Maybe Dad had been right after all and they should've just headed home. Celia and Luke were back to their moody selves. He knew he should be thankful for the fun times they'd enjoyed, but was it so bad to wish it could've lasted a little longer?

Out of the corner of his eye, he watched Celia close her sketch pad. She leaned toward Luke and him. *Oh, boy. Here goes round two for the knockout.*

"Story time."

His eyebrow raised. Well, that was unexpected.

"Sure." Luke motioned for her to sit at the table with them.

Not wanting to set off another angry mood, Austin decided the best course of action was to remain as still as possible.

Celia sank down next to Luke, then stared at her hands a moment before talking. "There once was an eighth-grade girl who was so excited to go to high school."

Holy mackerel! *Is she going to tell us what happened to make her change her M.O. to angry, depressed Celia?* His gaze shot toward Luke, who was intently watching their sister.

Celia kept her gaze down as she picked at her thumbnail. "This girl had two best friends who she did everything with. The three of them had so many plans for high school. They were going to meet new people, try new clubs, be outgoing . . . but most of all, they were going to do it all together." She paused for a moment. "The first few days of high school went pretty much according to plan, but then things fell apart. Especially excited about the back-to-school dance, the three friends meticulously planned what they would wear, spent hours getting ready, and arrived fashion-ably late. All went well, until this senior guy asked one of the friends to dance. She ended up dancing with him the whole night. She saw him again on Saturday night, and by the time Monday morning came around, she was lost to his charms and spent all her time with him and his group."

Celia's two best friends had always been Jordan and Skyler. *Which one would've dumped her friends for a guy?*

Celia's gaze shifted to the window. "This friend became like a stranger. Then the girl's other friend hooked up with a new crowd and invited the girl to join them one night at a home football game. The girl went, happy to have people to hang out with. But then the group decided to leave the game and head to a party. The girl wasn't so sure about going, but didn't want to be stuck at the game by herself, either. So, she went." Celia let out a slow breath, her focus remaining out-side. "The party was horrible. Drinking. Drugs. Cou-ples making out. No parents in sight. The girl pulled her friend aside and suggested they leave. The party wasn't too far from the girl's house. They could eas-ily walk home. But the friend said no. She refused to leave. The girl had a choice to make. Stay and try to protect her friend or leave. She said a prayer for guid-ance and then left. The friend began spending all her time with this new crowd and started ignoring the girl. Hurt, frustrated, and not sure who to be friends with, the girl decided to spend her lunch periods alone. Over time, she figured out if she wore dark colors and stayed out of the crowds, she would be ignored."

She finished and finally looked at Austin, then Luke.

Luke released his bottom lip, which had been clenched between his teeth. *"Whoa.* I didn't know."

Her eyes filled with tears. "And you know the worst part? My big brother wasn't there to support me."

Luke flinched.

She clenched her hands together. "When I needed you most, you ignored me, obviously embarrassed that I was your sister."

Whoa. Austin's eyes flicked between his older siblings.

Luke's eyes squeezed shut. When they opened, they were glistening with tears as well. "Celia, I'm . . . I'm sorry."

She wiped away a tear that slid down her face. "I had no one. Losing Jordan and Skyler was awful, but seeing you care more about what your friends thought than what I was going through was even worse."

The inspiring Christian song on the radio did nothing to lift the heavy silence that settled around them.

Luke let out a deep breath. "Celia, I had no idea why you began changing and isolating yourself. You're right, I should have tried to find out why." His Adam's apple bobbed as he swallowed. "I didn't realize until this trip how consumed with my friends I had become. I really am sorry."

"I guess I shouldn't have expected you to figure it out. You are a guy after all." She let out a little laugh which broke the tension.

Luke looked like he wanted to say more, but he kept quiet.

Guess it's my turn to say something. "Well, I'm glad you told us and that you're finally getting over them. I mean, just because your friends turned into total losers doesn't mean you should. Ow!" A sharp kick to the shin from Luke informed Austin that was not the thing to say.

Celia's eyes widened, then she laughed, her face softening. "Lately, I've been thinking the same thing. You know, it was so much fun hanging out with Britt and Mia, then Blake, and even you guys. I realized I missed that—having fun."

"I know what you mean." Luke's voice remained steady and calm. "So, do you have a plan for the coming year so it's not a repeat?"

"Maybe. Do you think it would be dumb if I tried out for the dance team?" She bit her thumb nail, watching Luke's reaction.

Luke's eyebrows arched. "Oh. Wow. Did not see that coming. No, I think that would be cool. But, um." He cleared his throat. "I think you have to be a pretty good dancer. Have you seen the dance team?"

Glad he had the guts to say it. Celia hadn't taken dance lessons since she was little. Austin couldn't picture her doing all those hip-hop dance moves.

Her worry turned into a smile. "I've been practicing on my own since January. It's amazing what you can learn watching videos."

"That's what you've been doing in your room?" And here Austin had thought she was just moping around, being all depressed.

Her cheeks turned a shade of pink. "I was binge-watching videos one day after Christmas and thought it looked fun to try."

Luke's eyes lit up like a lightbulb just went off in his brain. "No wonder you've been in such good shape during our hikes. That explains a lot." He ran his good hand along his cast. "Ya know, maybe I should change things up, as well."

"Because you can't play football?" Celia asked.

Luke knocked his knuckles against his cast. "Yeah."

Austin's gut clenched. *Will I ever stop feeling guilty?*

Their big brother cleared his throat. "Actually, that's not the only reason. I've been doing a lot of thinking lately. I don't even know when I became the sports guy. Sure, I like sports, but I used to have other interests. Somehow along the way, sports became the focus of my life. I don't have any friends besides ones in the jock crowd. Just like for you, hanging out with the people we've met on this trip has been eye-opening. Back home, it's so easy to get caught up in the little bubble we live in, but there are so many cool people out there and a lot of amazing things to experience." His good shoulder raised in a shrug. "I don't know, it just makes me want to shake it up a little and try new things."

Austin watched the back-and-forth between his siblings, for once not annoyed that they were talking about high school. Even though the conversation remained between them, he didn't feel excluded. He was glad they seemed to have figured some things out about their lives. Why couldn't he?

Celia's head tilted. "You don't like being part of the popular group? Do you know how many people would sell a body part just to be in that clique?"

"Yeah, but I'm not sure if any of them actually know or like me for me. And honestly, I don't really like who I am when I'm with them all the time. I mean, I was so absorbed that I didn't even know what was going on with you." Luke grimaced as he looked at Celia. "Who knows if they'd even want to hang out with me if I wasn't a jock."

She glanced at his cast. "I guess you'll find out."

"Yeah." Luke cocked his head. "Can I tell you how freeing it's been not to be tied to my phone? Being part of those group chats, making sure to say the right things, responding enough but not too much . . . it's a lot of pressure. I may never pick up my phone again."

"Yeah, right." Austin laughed but understood the feeling. Things had been so much better without the phones. But could they really ease off the devices once they were back home?

Celia glanced toward Mom and Dad, then shifted in her seat. "Did you guys ever read those Bible verses Grandma told us about? Ephesians 4 and 5?"

He and Luke shook their heads.

"Well, honestly, it took me a little while to understand why she wanted us to read them, but then it finally clicked. They are about distancing yourself from things that are bad and evil, and surrounding yourself with good people. It made me think about toxic friends and all the junk some kids see and do on their phones."

Like video games?

"Huh." Luke stared off to the right, his forehead creased. "I'll have to read them. It makes sense to distance yourself from temptations and stuff, but it's so hard to find people at school that have any kind of values."

"Tell me about it." Celia leaned back. "I stopped hanging out with Jordan and Skyler for those reasons. Everyone at school seems to be into stuff . . . That's why I ended up pulling the loner routine. I wonder where you find nice people?"

High school did not sound fun. Maybe he could skip a few years.

Luke tapped the table. "They've got to be out there somewhere. Probably also searching for new friends. Guess we'll have to keep an eye out for them. Anyway, I like your idea. Maybe I'll try something new this year too—since my football season is over."

Luke's words filled Austin with relief. Maybe if his brother found some other activity, he wouldn't blame Austin for ruining his football career. He glanced between his siblings. With new activities keeping them busy, Luke and Celia might actually be able to spend less time on their phones. But what about him? None of this changed his situation or how people saw him. He didn't really want to dive back into his games, but it still seemed better than the alternative—facing the burdensome expectations of others.

Celia tucked a strand of hair behind her ear. "You'll be great at anything you try."

"I'll come and cheer both of you on, no matter what you do," Austin announced. Maybe they could be the Three Musketeers again.

Celia grinned. "I'll hold you to that."

"Deal."

She pointed a finger at him. "That means you have to actually watch and not have your head buried in a game."

"No problem," he replied with more confidence than he felt.

Grandma

Harry,

Well, even though things did not exactly go according to plan, we actually found all the bags at Bryce. Can you believe they were all still there? Praise the Lord, our treasure is safe and sound. Now I just need to find the right time to tell them the rest of the story.

Grace

Chapter 28

Celia:
A Golden Opportunity

As Celia walked, her fingers tracing the thin white vein that coursed through the red rocks of the narrow canyon, she replayed her talk with the boys. Where'd the courage come from to share with them what had happened with Jordan and Skyler? She shivered remembering back to the painful stab of rejection she'd felt from the two sources she'd always turned to when she'd needed help—her big brother and God. Turned out neither of them had actually given up on her.

Grandma had been right, as usual. God hadn't abandoned her. His no to her prayers in the fall had really been a gentle push, leading her to something else. She still wasn't quite sure what that was but felt like she was finally on the right path. She'd have to thank Grandma for the advice. Not to mention those Bible verses she'd suggested which had gotten Celia thinking about the choices she'd been making. She'd never really thought about choosing friends based on their values but now saw how important similar beliefs could be. Guess locating a few like-minded friends should be the goal of the coming school year. Wonder where those elusive new pals were hiding? Hopefully, God would keep leading her in the right direction.

Even more shocking than opening up to her brothers was their reaction. Especially Luke's. She had been sure he'd think her idea about joining the dance team was dumb, but he'd been surprisingly supportive. It was amazing how relieved and unburdened she felt—like her guardian angel had hoisted a massive boulder off her shoulders. Maybe things were finally looking up.

"Whatcha thinking?"

She glanced back to find Luke watching her.

"I know what she's thinking." Austin plunged into the conversation before she had a chance to answer. "She's trying to figure out which colored pencil to use when she gets back to the camper to start drawing this place."

She grinned. "Wrong. I'm thinking that I can't believe we found a canyon even more beautiful than Bryce." Maybe it wasn't exactly what had been on her mind, but it was true. The parks they'd visited kept surprising her. These narrow paths winding through the swirly patterned walls of the slot canyons were unreal;

in some places, they were barely wide enough to walk through. The way the sun filtered in from the narrow openings above, highlighting the natural stripes of the curved sandstone, reminded her of ocean waves.

"Yeah. This place is incredible." Luke turned to his little brother. "How about you, Austin? What're you thinking as you walk through here?"

Austin snapped a pic with Mom's phone. "That's easy. I'm thinking how much it would bite to be stuck in here when a flash flood hits."

A shiver ran down Celia's spine. Their guide had explained how flash floods had formed these unusual canyons—water swept through the narrow passages, carving into the sandstone. Not hard to believe the stories of drownings. There would be nowhere to go if water blasted through here.

"Luke, what are you thinking?" She shot the question back to him.

He rubbed his jawline. "Honestly? I wish this trip would last longer and that we weren't on the way home."

When'd you learn to read minds, big brother? It was crazy to think about how much had changed. Before they'd left on this summer adventure, she would've bet money that at this point in the journey they would all be counting the moments until the torturous, forced family vacation ended.

Austin handed Mom's phone to Celia. She snapped a few more pictures, hoping the photos captured the unique beauty of the canyon, and realized her little brother was right—she was pondering just how to sketch the flowing serenity of this place.

"Come on." From the lead position of their single-file line, Dad called back to them. "There's a wider spot up ahead. Our guide said he could take our family photo there."

They all bunched together and smiled as the guide took a few shots of the group. Without a doubt, this would be one of Celia's favorite family photos ever. Years from now, she'd look at the picture and be swept back in time to this moment.

"Okay, ready to go?" Dad asked after they thanked their guide for the great tour. "It's been a long day. Let's get to our campsite."

"So, what was everyone's favorite part of the day?" Mom inquired as they trekked toward the parking lot.

Celia didn't hesitate for a moment. "These slot canyons, for sure."

"I may have to go with Horseshoe Bend." Luke was also quick with his answer. "That was pretty amazing."

Ooh, good choice. They'd stood on the edge of a towering cliff, peering down through the canyon to the Colorado River where it had carved a path around a rocky spire, creating a horseshoe shape. Pretty spectacular.

Grandma wrapped her arm around Celia's. "My favorite part of the day was seeing the kids get along so well and enjoy the trip."

She patted Grandma's hand. "I still can't get over how all these canyons we've seen are so vastly different. It's truly amazing."

"Yeah." Austin kicked a small rock, sending it skidding across the parking lot. "Thanks for bringing us on this trip."

Dad froze, then turned to Mom. "Did he just thank us for this vacation?"

Mom grabbed his arm. "Keep walking and pretend you didn't hear, before he denies it."

Celia caught Grandma's sly little smile—like her devious plan had come to fruition.

"But anyway, you all are wrong." Austin sent another stone skittering away. "The dam was by far the best thing we saw today."

"The Glen Canyon Dam?" Dad's wide eyes zeroed in on him. "You mean the one you complained about going to visit? The one that I *forced* you to see and 'took all your fun away' to do so? That dam?"

Austin rolled his eyes. "You know you're not nearly as funny as you think you are?"

Grandma laughed. "The dam was fascinating."

"I know!" Austin spun around to face her. "The river is just all normal on the one side, but on the other is this unbelievable lake that fills all those valleys between the mountains. How'd they ever think to do that? So cool."

The kid they'd had to practically lure into the building was the same one they hadn't been able to drag out. He'd been so fascinated by the whole thing that he hadn't stopped pummeling the park ranger with questions. The three males in the family hadn't been able to get enough of that place.

Austin kept talking to no one in particular. "It's so weird to think about how Lake Powell is a flooded canyon. Think about how deep that lake must be."

Dad tapped the bill of Austin's baseball hat. "Then you'll be happy to know that tomorrow we'll take a boat tour to get a feel of the lake."

Austin readjusted his cap. "Well, I don't mean to *rock the boat,* but I can't wait to explore the fingers of the lake tomorrow."

Luke groaned at the pun.

Austin glanced over his shoulder. "Hey, don't *harbor* a grudge at my witty brilliance."

Before he could add any more not-funny jokes, Celia redirected the conversation. "Going to the lake sounds like a perfect plan for tomorrow." She couldn't wait to zip across the lake with the red canyon walls surrounding them.

"The boat stops at a cool place for lunch, where we can hike to the natural rock formation, Rainbow Arch." Dad huffed out of breath, as they approach the RV. "Here we are."

Mom pulled open the camper door. "Good. Since we aren't stopping at Arches National Park, I want to see the one here."

Arches National Park? *Hmm . . . what were the chances of talking them into extending this trip?*

- - - X - - -

The boat ride, though, was not at all what she'd expected. Being stuck on a large tourist rig with several busloads of other people was not living up to Celia's visions of ripping through the water in a speed boat. But even though the ride to their destination putzed along at an excruciatingly slow pace, it was beautiful. The tour guide rambled on with facts about the lake and surrounding area, but Celia zoned out the loud-speaker and scrutinized the canyon walls, trying to sear the images into her brain. The hues ranged from off-white, to gray, to shades of pink and red—the stripes of color, a visual geological history of the area.

Finally, they docked at their stopping point for the next few hours.

"Where are we eating lunch?" Austin blurted, not-so-patiently waiting for Grandma to stand up.

Dad glanced at his watch. "Want to eat here by the water or hike to the arch and eat there?"

"Whatever *floats your boat,*" Grandma answered then, looking very impressed with herself, winked at Austin.

Austin rewarded her with a high five. "A pun! Nice! Did you cave under the *pier* pressure?" He snorted a little laugh.

Celia bit her bottom lip to keep from laughing. *No need to encourage him.*

"But seriously," Austin said. "Let's hike first."

Her little brother's answer came as a surprise. He was usually anxious for feeding time.

"Perfect. It's a *ferry* impressive plan." Mom extended her hand, awaiting her high five.

Celia rolled her eyes, then looked at Luke, who was shaking his head. Time to get moving before they were subject to more of these awful puns. "Shall we go?"

"Sure." Dad turned to Grandma. "Feel up to walking that far, Mom?"

She clapped her hands together. "I'm ready."

Austin turned his baseball cap around. "Hey, do you mind if Celia, Luke, and I go ahead and meet you there?"

"That's fine," Mom answered. "Just be careful."

Austin waved a hand in reply, then scurried down the ramp. Celia and Luke followed. Within minutes, they passed the slow-moving pack of migrating passengers.

Celia took a swig from her water bottle to cool herself from the stifling desert heat. "It's getting warm. Hopefully, Grandma can make it."

Luke glanced over his shoulder. "Think we should wait for them?"

Austin shook his head. "Nah. Besides, I wanted to talk to you two about something."

What's he up to? His mischievous grin caused a ripple of unease to run through Celia.

Luke wiped the sweat from his forehead. "What's up?"

Austin bit his lower lip as if he was trying to contain his smile. He didn't succeed.

Celia nudged him. "Come on. The suspense is killing me." It really wasn't, but the kid looked like he was about to burst.

Austin's eyes brightened. "Well, I was thinking all night about something that Luke said yesterday." He glanced around as if making sure no one was listening. Not much chance of that since their brisk pace had left the other passengers in the dust. The desolate trail remained free from eavesdroppers except for maybe a manner-less lizard or curious bird.

Apparently satisfied that they were, in fact, alone, he continued. "Remember when you said you were bummed that we're on our way home and our adventure will be over soon?"

Luke's left eyebrow arched. "Yeah. So?"

"Well, what if it didn't have to end?"

Celia had to admit it, he'd gotten her attention. Sounded like he was up for extending the trip as well. "Go on."

Austin slowed his pace, shrugged off his backpack and unzipped it. "We had such a fun time searching for Grandma's hidden items. What if we do the same?" He pulled out the bags of coins and held them in the air.

Celia stopped walking. "Wait. What are you thinking?"

Austin's face beamed. "Let's bury them. Grandma said the coins were ours. Just think, years from now, we can come back with our kids and see if the bags are still here." His eyes darted between her and Luke.

Celia stared at his face, then down at the bags in his hand. *Huh. Why didn't I think of that?*

Austin's eyes opened wide. "Come on, whaddaya think?"

Her gaze slid toward Luke. "It would be kind of fun to have a future adventure."

Luke grinned. "I like it. Let's do it."

Chapter 29

LUKE:
A HAIL MARY PASS

Luke stared at the playing cards in his hand. *Arrgh.* Holding the cards in his left hand with the stupid cast that wrapped around his thumb certainly turned an enjoyable activity into a tedious task. As he struggled, Dad whistled along to the newly purchased cowboy CD that played in the background—Austin's choice of music for the morning.

"I have no idea which national park I liked best." Austin scanned the photos on Mom's phone, while Luke attempted to extract the desired card without dropping the rest.

"I agree." Mom peered over Austin's shoulder to view the pictures. "Every place we visited was spectacular."

Grandma smiled. "I'm so thankful you all agreed to come on this trip with me. It has meant so much."

Dad stretched his arms above his head. "It was also nice for the kids to put their phones down and for us all to spend some time together."

Mom leaned against Dad, who lowered an arm around her shoulder. "Yes, we've all gotten so caught up in the busyness of life. We needed this reminder of our priorities."

Austin slammed his hand on the table. "Hey! We should make this an annual trip. Every summer, we could check out a different national park. Kinda like Grandma and her family did."

"That's actually a good idea." Celia ruffled Austin's hair.

Luke nodded as he continued concentrating on the task at hand. "I'd be down for that."

Mom snuggled closer to Dad. "I guess we have our summer vacations planned for the foreseeable future."

"Works for me." Dad turned to his mom. "Feel like joining us again?"

Grandma smiled. "I can't think of a better way to spend my summers. In fact, my diary reminded me of a few other amazing places we could visit." Her gaze traveled to her loved ones around the table. "I'm glad you all enjoyed the trip. Spending time together as a family is very important. And you know, siblings are special friends that are in your lives forever."

Celia nudged Austin. "Whether you like it or not."

He stuck out his tongue in reply.

Luke finally managed to successfully wiggle the card out of his hand and dropped it on the table, slightly missing his intended target. *Close enough.* "It really has been a fantastic trip."

Celia reached out, placing Luke's card on the discard pile. "Yeah, it's been great. And thanks, Mom, for letting us use your phone. It was nice taking photos for the memories."

Grandma chose a card from the draw pile. "Right, and now you can always remember the adventure."

"Yep." Austin carelessly tossed a card, which skimmed across the table. "Until we come again."

Dad rescued the errant card and placed it on the pile. "You never know. Maybe you will return someday."

"Oh, we'll definitely return again. We made sure of that." The way Austin rearranged his cards with such ease filled Luke with envy.

Amazing, the little things you take for granted.

Grandma lowered her cards. "How did you make sure of it?"

"The same way you did." Austin grinned, wiggling his eyebrows.

Grandma's eyes widened. "What do you mean?"

Austin leaned forward, eager to share the news. "We had so much fun searching for the coins, we decided to do the same thing with our kids someday."

"You . . . *hid* the bags?" Grandma's face paled. Not the reaction they had expected.

Austin tilted his head to the side. "Yeah. Why?"

Grandma suddenly dropped back in her chair, her right hand clutching her chest.

"Mom!" Dad's cards scattered across the table as he lunged toward his mother.

- - - X - - -

"What if I just killed Grandma?" Austin whispered as the ambulance transporting their grandmother pulled out of the campsite. The police car taking Mom and Dad to the hospital followed along.

Luke tore his gaze from the flashing lights to look at his brother. Tears pooled in the kid's worried eyes.

Celia wrapped an arm around Austin's shoulders. "Don't say that."

"But my great idea just gave her a heart attack." His voice quivered. The kid who was so great during the crisis in Bryce Canyon was melting before their eyes.

Celia steered Austin toward the picnic table.

Luke lowered himself to sit across from them, knowing he needed to step up. His younger brother had helped him during his moment of need—now it was time to return the favor. "Celia's right. First of all, we don't know that she's having a heart attack. And besides, we all agreed to the idea, so this is not on you."

Austin buried his head in his hands. "Seeing her like that was so awful."

Can't disagree there. Grandma's pale face, the way she clutched her chest, her wide, scared eyes. None of them would be able to shake those images for a while.

Celia rubbed Austin's back and set her questioning eyes on Luke. *Like I know what to do. Sometimes being the oldest bites.* He turned away.

They sat in silence for a few minutes until Celia finally broke the somber moment. "Let's pray." She led them in an Our Father and a Hail Mary, then added a few words about watching over Grandma and keeping her safe.

The prayer helped, but stress lines still crossed Celia's face. "I have no idea why Grandma freaked so badly. She said the items were our souvenirs."

Luke wedged a finger under his cast, trying desperately to reach an itch. "She's sentimental. She probably wanted to show them to Harry."

Celia shrugged in response.

Momentarily relieved of the annoying itch, Luke looked toward the shimmering lake surrounded by the flat, red mesas. An idea zipped through his mind. "Hey, maybe instead of sitting around here, waiting and worrying, we should go retrieve the bags."

Austin peered at him through red-rimmed eyes. "But how could we go get them now? That tour boat only heads out once a day."

True. Guess his game plan was a little faulty.

"What about jet skis?" Celia's somber face transformed with a slight twinkle in her eye. "We wanted to try them out, anyway. And Dad already has them reserved."

The worry in Austin's face relaxed. "That's a great idea." He looked at Luke. "What do you think?"

It beats sitting around here. "Let's do it."

- - - X - - -

As they made their way through the narrow channel between the marina and the open water, Luke adjusted to the awkwardness of clutching the handlebars with his cumbersome cast. Luckily, accelerating only required squeezing the trigger with two fingers. He visualized the journey ahead of them as they slowly made their way through the no-wake zone. Thankfully, the guy at the rental shop had helped them navigate a map of the lake on Mom's phone. He had pointed out their current location and where the boat dock near Rainbow Bridge arch could be found. With so many canyon fingers in the lake, it was easy to see how people could get lost out there. How did people survive before modern technology and GPS?

The moment they passed the last buoy in the channel, Austin gunned his machine and flew past them. He didn't travel far, though, before cranking the handlebars and whipping in circles at top speed. Luke glanced at Celia, expecting her to roll her eyes at Austin's antics, but instead, she raised an eyebrow and cocked her head to the side.

Luke nodded, accepting the unspoken challenge, and soon they joined their younger brother, spinning donuts in the water. The wind and spray of the water blowing across his face somehow created a sense of invincibility. When was the last time he'd felt this free?

They chased each other and raced around the enormous lake for a while before Celia waved them to a stop.

She adjusted her ponytail, pulling her hair tighter against her head. "I guess we'd better get moving."

A stab of guilt hit Luke. They'd been having so much fun, he'd briefly forgotten about Grandma and the reason they were on the lake.

Austin sighed. "Yeah, okay."

Celia led the way—Austin close behind her, with Luke bringing up the rear. As they skimmed across the water, Luke scanned the scenery around him, admiring the sandstone cliffs that ranged in color from reds and browns to creams and yellows. In some places, thin layers of stone had broken away from the cliffs, resulting in odd, layered stacks that made him hungry for Pringles chips.

As they continued their journey, Luke realized just how happy he was. Despite being worried about Grandma and suffering a broken arm, he was happier than he'd been in a long time. Time to face the truth—with each passing day, it became more evident that there were things in his life that probably needed changing. It was like he'd been on a mundane carousel, unable to get off. Stuck in a rut with the same group of people. People who, if he was honest with himself, might not be the best for him. But meeting new friends on this trip had shown him there were a lot of cool people out there—people who might actually want to get to know him and not just hang with him because he was part of a certain group or on the football team.

A cramp in his injured hand served as a painful reminder of his current situation. Well, since his high school football career was trashed, now would be an excellent time to reinvent himself. Just like Celia. *But what do I want to do?* Checking out colleges that offered engineering programs was one thing that had suddenly jumped to the top of his to-do list. All those amazing structures they'd seen on this trip made him realize he'd love to help create such things. But he also needed something to do for fun. Someway to make new friends—because he wasn't sure how many of his current group would want to hang out with the new and improved Luke. All he'd focused on in high school had been sports. Grandma mentioned that God could use their disappointments to lead people in a new direction. So, what had he wanted to do but hadn't had time for? He scanned the natural beauty surrounding them and thought about the church youth group's annual camping trip. That event had always sounded like a blast, but he'd never been able to go due to football practice. *Maybe this is the year to make it happen.*

A spray of cool water hit his face. Back when he had been preparing for Confirmation, one of the things they discussed was how to live your life for Christ. Was he doing that? Not really. Those verses from Ephesians that Celia had mentioned came to mind. He really needed to read them for himself. So, what was pulling him away from Christ? Certain friends? Sports? Technology? All of it seemed so innocent, but were some things in his life becoming more important than his faith? Scary thought. *Definitely time to refocus priorities.*

Lost in his thoughts, he didn't notice right away when Celia stopped. He nearly flew right past her.

He let off the gas and pulled up next to her. "What's up? Still headed in the right direction?" They'd passed so many little inlets that all looked alike. Good thing for the navigational help of the GPS. Without it, they'd never find the right passages to take.

Austin slowly circled them on his jet ski, causing them to bob up and down. *He never can sit still.*

Celia tucked her windblown hair behind her ear. "We're about halfway there, but I don't like the look of those clouds."

For the first time, Luke noticed the dark horizon. He must've been pretty deep in his own head to have missed the darkening sky. "Hopefully, they'll blow off in another direction. We'll have to keep an eye on them."

Austin swung into view as he finished his loop around them. "Let's keep moving. We can sit out a rainstorm at the dock."

Celia gave a quick nod, then started off again.

This time, Luke spent less time admiring the beauty of the canyon and more time assessing the dark clouds that were not dissipating. As they rolled closer, the wind picked up, creating waves. The once-smooth water churned. Their gliding journey across the smooth-as-glass lake became a bouncing passage through rough water. Luke tried to steer around the wells, but the jarring crashes made it hard to control the jet ski. His injured arm ached from the jolts.

A sudden flash of lightning and crash of thunder left him breathless. Celia and Austin both stopped their slow forward progress as well. They were in danger.

Everyone knew it wasn't safe to be on the water in a lightning storm.

Stark fear shone in Austin's huge eyes. Celia studied the phone, then aimed a finger toward the right. "We need to get off the lake. See that little inlet? Maybe we can wait out the storm there."

Another flash of lightning emphasized the point—they didn't have a lot of choices. Luke followed Celia into a narrow finger of water. *Where are we going to find a spot to park the jet skis?* Most of the lake was surrounded by the canyon cliffs. Meaning few beaches. If they abandoned the lake for safety from the storm, the jet skis might float away.

Okay, God, we could use a hand here.

As the rain intensified, Luke squinted as he watched Celia bounce around the choppy water. He followed closely as she rounded a few bends, then slowed. The inlet ended in a patch of tall grasses growing up through the water. With any luck, the thick tufts would keep the jet skis from drifting. Another boom of thunder accompanied by a blinding flash of light meant it didn't matter—they were out of options. *This will have to do.* The skies opened. In the midst of a torrential downpour, the siblings pushed their rides into the reeds as close to shore as possible, then scrambled away from the water.

Luke surveyed the area then motioned for his siblings to follow him toward a groove in the rocks. It was more of an overhang than a cave, but at least it provided a bit of shelter.

Celia shivered as she sat down. "It was s-so hot earlier. How can it be so co-cold all of a sudden?"

Sheets of rain pounded onto the lake. "Hopefully this won't last long. Are we close to the dock?" Luke propped his waterproof cast on his knee in hopes of stopping the throbbing.

Celia reached into a pocket and pulled out the phone. "Oh no."

The panic in her eyes revealed everything he needed to know. "Let me guess. The phone got wet and isn't working."

She let out a long breath. "Yeah. But I think there were only a few fingers between here and the dock."

Austin shifted his feet. "Um, guys."

"Yeah?" *What now?* The tone of Austin's voice worried him.

"Any idea how much longer the jet skis run after the low-gas alarm starts beeping?"

Celia gasped. "Are you serious?"

Rivulets of water slid down Austin's face when he nodded.

"How long has that been happening?" Despair flooded through Luke.

Austin bit his lip. "For a little while."

Celia groaned. "If yours is low, that means ours must be, too."

Not far from the arch was a marina where they had planned to fill up, but what happened if Austin's jet ski ran out of gas before they reached it? Could they tow him? Maybe they needed to leave his machine here and have Austin ride with one of them? *Could things get any worse? Grandma's in the hospital. We're stuck out here in the middle of a storm with no phone, our vehicles are low on gas, and no one knows where we are.*

Austin wrapped his arms around his knees. "I guess Operation Coin Retrieval has hit another snag."

Luke's jaw clenched. *Does everything have to be a game with him?*

"But, hey, I thought of something as we were riding." Austin pushed a chunk of wet hair from his face. "An Austin original. Why was the sandstone banned from the rock band?" He glanced between his siblings, then grinned. "Because it was too flaky! Get it? Because the sandstone flakes apart so easily?"

Enough with the jokes! "Don't you *get* it?" Luke's frustration about everything—his arm, his uncertain future, Grandma, their dire circumstances—boiled over, and he snapped. "This is not some stupid video game adventure. We are in serious trouble. We have no phone or GPS. We are stuck in this desolate place, and no one knows where we are. If we run out of gas, we're screwed."

Luke's anger continued to brew as they sat in silence, surrounded by lightning, thunder, pounding rain, and whipping wind. No one uttered a word as the minutes slowly ticked by.

"Story time." Austin's voice was a muffled whisper, almost lost to the sounds of nature's fury.

You've got to be kidding me!

Luke opened his mouth ready to skewer Austin with the fact that this was not the time or place for whatever stupid thing he was about to say, but the look in the kid's eyes stopped him cold. It was the same wild, frenzied look that Coach got when he was about to tear the team apart after a loss.

Austin stood and shoved a pointed finger toward their faces. "You guys think I spend all my time playing video games. And I guess I do when we're together. But do you know why? You probably never even stopped to wonder. It's because you guys never want to do anything with me. Ever. You won't watch any show or movie that I want to watch. You won't ever hang out with me anymore. We used to have a blast together." He sucked in a breath of air before continuing. "I always thought you guys were the coolest, and I just wanted to do whatever you did. Maybe you thought of me as the annoying younger brother, but I thought we had fun together. Then you go off to high school and suddenly want nothing to do with me. You always act like I'm such a nuisance. Do you know how lonely that is? You would never talk to me. You completely ignored me. So, I played video games for something to do, and you know what? The characters in those games never made me feel useless and unwanted."

He turned and stomped away from the safety of their shelter.

Whoa. Luke watched in stunned silence as the downpour swallowed Austin from view, then he turned to Celia for her reaction.

"Wow." She bit her lower lip. "He's right, though. We used to be close." Her eyes squeezed shut. "We all have stuff going on in our lives that we never share with each other. How'd we get to this point?"

His shoulders sagged. *What a disaster.* "Yeah. It's amazing how you get so involved in your own problems and don't even see that others are dealing with stuff, too." *Some brother I've been.*

She turned in the direction Austin stormed off. "Do we let him cool off?"

Luke shook his head. "No. We need to go after him and fix this."

Chapter 30

Austin:
For the Win

The rain pounded down around him. Not one dry inch remained anywhere on Austin's shivering body. *Maybe stalking off wasn't the brightest idea ever.* Still, there was no way he could've stayed with those two for another moment. His siblings never thought of anyone but themselves. *Lord, why are they so awful? You were lucky You didn't have any siblings.*

But there was at least one bright spot to his current miserable situation. The center of the storm seemed to have passed. The claps of thunder had lost their bone-jarring power and were no longer in sync with the flash and streaks of deadly light.

"Hey."

Geesh! He jumped, not having heard his siblings approach. He glared in response, thankful the rain had washed away any evidence of his tears.

Luke sat down, keeping his distance, while Celia remained standing, her arms wrapped around her chest.

Luke blinked away the water that streamed down his face. "Hey, we're sorry if we've been ignoring you. I got so caught up in high school and being in the right group and sports that I didn't realize I was pulling away from you."

"Yeah." Celia finally knelt down between the boys. "Things with my friends were so bad, and I tried to deal with it on my own. I should have told you guys about it instead of closing up."

"We're sorry it seemed like we didn't want to hang out with you anymore." Luke's expression seemed sincere, but did he mean it?

Might as well get everything out in the open. "It's not just that. You have no idea what it's like living in your shadows."

His siblings exchanged a confused look.

Did he really have to spell it out for them? "I hate that people don't see me for me. You guys still think of me as your annoying little brother. And every teacher or coach I've ever had compared me to the two of you. Even our priest and youth group leader. I'm so sick of hearing what a gifted athlete Luke is. 'He was a natural leader, blah, blah, blah.' And they can never shut up about what a brilliant student Celia was. 'Such a joy to have in class. I could always count on her.' *Whatever.*" He hugged his knees, resting his head on his arms as he curled into a ball. "It's easier to just stay away from it all."

After a moment, Celia reached out to touch his arm. "Really? I had no idea."

"Agreed. That's totally warped," Luke added.

Austin raised one shoulder in a half-hearted shrug, afraid to say anything that would bring on the tears again. He'd been praying that his siblings would realize how he felt, but had it been worth everything crumbling apart for that to happen?

Celia scooched closer and wrapped an arm around him. "I guess Luke and I still have been treating you as our baby brother and didn't notice how much you've changed. I don't know about Luke, but the other night I sure saw a new side to you. The way you took charge of the situation when Luke fell—that was pretty amazing."

"Absolutely," Luke agreed. "If you hadn't been there and helped me with my arm, I don't know what I would've done. You knew just what to do and kept me calm until help arrived. It was impressive."

Any chance they meant it?

Celia rested her head against his shoulder. "We're really sorry."

"Completely. Hey, maybe we can start spending more time together," Luke offered.

Doubtful. There was nothing Austin would like more than that, but he sure wasn't going to admit it— yet. They needed to be punished a little longer. Instead of making eye contact, he focused his attention to the lake. As the rain began to let up, the water came into view.

"Oh no!" He jumped up and pointed to where the jet skis were floating, having escaped from their nest of grasses.

"Great," Luke grumbled. With his good hand, he brushed back his soaked hair. "What else can go wrong?"

Austin didn't wait to hear Celia's response. If they lost their transportation, they were in serious trouble. He needed to act. With a flying leap off the cliff, he plunged into the water.

"Austin!" Celia screamed as he swam toward the drifting jet skis.

While he moved through the water, two thoughts came to mind. First, the water felt way colder than it did before. And second, swimming with a life vest on was less than productive.

Finally, he made it to the closest jet ski, which happened to be his. He scrambled on, started it up, and drove back toward the grassy inlet. The incessant low-on-gas alarm frazzled his nerves like a terminal countdown in one of his video games. The extra reminder of their dire situation was not helpful. By the time he arrived in the cove, his siblings were waiting.

"Celia, climb on. I'll take you over to your ride, then come back for Luke."

Celia glanced at Luke, then splashed through the water and climbed on behind Austin, wrapping her arms around his waist. He was surprised by how far the other two jet skis had already drifted by the time they reached them. Austin edged his machine next to Celia's, and she scrambled over.

Austin veered his jet ski back to the inlet to retrieve Luke, trying to ignore the annoying beeps. *I get it; you're low on fuel.* By the time they returned, Luke's ride bobbed noticeably further from the cliff where they had been sitting. The warning signal now emanating from Celia's jet ski matched his own. Austin's heart plummeted. *Just what we need, another problem.*

Luke settled himself onto his jet ski, then looked back at Austin. "I thought you were insane jumping off the cliff and swimming after them, but thank goodness you did. The longer we waited, the further they would've drifted."

Austin pushed a chunk of wet hair out of his eyes to get a better look at the cliff he'd leapt from. "I didn't really think it through; I just reacted."

Luke's head tilted. "You know, you're amazingly chill in stressful situations."

Celia nodded. "You really are. Who knew the little boy who couldn't make it through the night when we camped in the backyard would become such a *warrior*? Okay, let's try to make it to the Dangling Rope Marina and refuel."

Warrior? Still not ready to completely forgive and forget, Austin sped away, hiding his smile.

The sky turned blue once again as the sudden, horrible storm moved on. The red rocks blurred past them as they desperately tried to reach their destination. Of course, without a working phone, they were mostly guessing where the marina was located.

Then it happened. The motor of Austin's jet ski made a sickening sound, sputtered, then stalled. Luke, who was bringing up the rear, flew past. The telltale warning beep now also sounded from Luke's machine. Luke glanced over his shoulder. Austin sliced at his neck, signaling that his machine was dead. Luke nodded then zoomed ahead to catch Celia. Soon, they both returned to their stranded brother.

"Should we try to make it?" Luke suggested. "Maybe we can bring some gas back to you."

Celia shook her head. "Mine's making a weird sound. I think I'm running on fumes."

They bobbed in the middle of the lake—not a soul in sight. It could be hours before someone came along to offer assistance. They'd eventually be rescued, since patrol boats came by occasionally, but who knew how long that would take?

Luke glanced in the direction they were headed. "I'm not sure it's a good idea for me to keep going alone. I don't know exactly where the dock is, or if my jet ski would even make it. Then I'd be stranded as well, but nowhere near you."

Celia closed her eyes, then nodded. "Yeah, better to stick together."

"Just the way it should be," Luke replied with a crooked grin.

- - - X - - -

Austin had been bravely leading the way down the hospital corridor, but suddenly all courage drained away. He stopped outside their grandmother's room, fear overpowering the worry that had propelled him forward.

Luke briefly glanced at his brother, then pushed his way into the room. Celia followed along, pausing briefly to squeeze Austin's hand. The small encouragement was greatly appreciated.

Please, Lord, give me the strength to deal with whatever we find.

After a deep breath, Austin warily stepped into the room and peeked around the curtain that hid the bed from his view. Lying in the middle of the hospital bed, Grandma's small frame seemed even more frail than usual. At least her color had improved slightly. He shot up a prayer of thanks.

With a sigh of relief, he glanced around the room. No Mom or Dad.

Grandma gave a tired smile as she set down the pen in her hand. "This is a nice surprise. I didn't expect to see you three this afternoon."

Celia sank into a chair next to the bed. "We were worried and didn't want to keep sitting around, waiting for news."

"Well, I'm glad you came." Grandma's soft voice sounded as weak as she looked. "Your folks are down in the cafeteria getting a bite to eat."

Luke perched on the foot of her bed, making himself comfortable. Austin longed to approach but couldn't shake the unnerving vibe that hospitals always gave him, so he stayed firmly planted at the foot of the bed.

Grandma's gaze settled on her youngest grandson. "I'm sure I gave you quite a scare."

What an understatement. Time to face the truth. "Did you have a heart attack?"

Her head slowly rolled from side to side. "No. They ran a few tests and believe it was a stress-related incident."

Thank you, God. Her words offered the comfort he desperately needed, so he finally approached and gently lowered himself on the opposite edge of her bed from Luke. "Thank goodness. We were afraid we'd killed you."

"No. It was just a shock and a bit distressing to hear that you had buried the bags."

"Well, worry no more." Celia shrugged her backpack from her shoulder and pulled out the treasure bags. "We recovered them."

Grandma's eyes lit up. She pressed her hands to her cheeks. "Where were they?" She made the sign of the cross.

The look on her face was worth the difficulty and frustration of the afternoon. "We buried them near Rainbow Arch yesterday."

She glanced around the bed at each of them. "At the arch? That was quite far away. How did you get back there?"

Luke ran his right hand through his hair. "It's a long story."

"From the way you look, I'm guessing it's an interesting one as well, one I can't wait to hear." Grandma relaxed further into her pillow.

Austin glanced at his siblings, taking in their disheveled and dirty appearances. "Yeah, I guess we do look rather ragged."

Celia lowered the bags to her lap, then tried to run her fingers through her matted hair. "Well, since you seemed so upset, we knew we had to get them back."

Austin tried to brush a smudge of dirt off his shorts. His effort just made the streak grow. "I'm sorry we buried them. It was my dumb idea. They belong to you, and we didn't have a right to take them."

"As soon as the ambulance pulled away from the campsite, we came up with a plan," Luke explained. "One that called for jet skis."

"But . . ." Celia continued, "it turns out it wasn't our best idea ever."

"Yeah, those machines are a blast, but they don't have very large fuel tanks." Not wanting to relive the emotional drama of the day, Austin excluded the big fight from the retelling.

Luke grimaced. "And we maybe should have checked the weather before heading out."

Grandma's eyes grew increasingly larger with each new revelation. "Let me get this straight—the three of you were stranded in the middle of Lake Powell on jet skis?"

Celia leaned back in her chair. "In a lightning storm."

"We sat there bobbing around in the middle of the lake forever." Austin couldn't help but notice the little twinkle of intrigue in his grandmother's eyes. *Could their crazy adventure somehow be making her feel bet-*

ter? Well, if that was the case, he wasn't going to ruin the excitement by admitting how scared he'd been.

Luke stood and stretched. "God must have heard our desperate prayers, because eventually a huge houseboat came our way." He pulled a chair from the corner of the room over to the bed and took a seat.

Austin grinned, remembering how furiously they'd yelled and waved, trying to get the attention of the occupants of the boat. The oblivious passengers had their music blaring and couldn't hear the calls for help. At first, they just waved back a friendly greeting to the siblings' frantic arm gestures.

Celia chuckled, probably remembering the scene as well. "Once they finally realized we were stranded, they towed us to that little dock near Rainbow Bridge Arch."

"Then came the tough part—running on the wet trail all the way to where we had buried the bags." Austin grabbed his waist, still remembering the painful side ache.

"Did the houseboat take you back to the Wahweap Marina by the campground?"

Austin's eyes narrowed. *Is Grandma's coloring improving? She really is enjoying this.* "No. But they were so intrigued by our story that they waited for us to retrieve our treasure, then towed us to the Dangling Rope Marina for fuel."

Luke leaned forward, his cast resting on his thigh. "The guy who refueled the tanks shared with us the helpful information that if we kept our speeds even and didn't screw around doing donuts"—he shot a conspiratorial grin Austin's way—"we could actually make it back to the boat rental dock at Wahweap."

Grandma's eyes brimmed with emotion. "I can't believe you went through all that for me." She blinked back the tears. "And how did you get here?"

Celia pulled a tissue from the box on the nightstand and handed it to Grandma. "We were telling one of the workers at the dock all about you and our crazy afternoon, and she offered to drive us here."

Grandma dabbed at her eyes. "Oh my, that is quite the tale. I'm so glad you came by. I feel so much better already."

"Oh!" They all turned to see Mom peek her head around the curtain. "What are you all doing here?"

Dad followed her into the room. His jaw twitched as he scanned each of them, not missing their drowned-rat appearances from the torrential rainstorm.

Austin glanced at his siblings and Grandma, waiting for someone to answer Mom's question, but no one seemed ready to rehash the afternoon's adventure. It appeared they all might be in agreement that the folks probably couldn't handle the truth right now. Definitely a tale for another day.

"We tried to call with an update, but you must have turned the phone off." Dad didn't even try to hide his annoyance.

Celia's gaze shifted toward the window. "Yeah, the phone stopped working."

Smooth answer. Plenty of time to fess up later.

"You could have used one of your phones since it was an emergency," Mom pointed out.

Again, no one shared that they totally would have broken their pact and used one of their phones to call and check on Grandma, but since they'd never made it back to the campground after being rescued, they hadn't had a chance.

Celia once again held up the bags. "We thought we'd stop by and let Grandma know that we retrieved the items."

Austin swallowed the lump in his throat, then bravely looked Dad in the eye. "We're sorry for causing Grandma's stress. We should have known she would want to show the treasure to Harry. It was wrong of us to take them and bury them without checking with her first."

Dad crossed his arms. "I'm glad you learned your lesson."

"Thank you for going back and getting the bags for Grandma." Mom rubbed Austin's back.

"It was an adventure." Probably the truest understatement he'd ever uttered.

Celia smiled. "A sibling adventure."

Luke grinned. "And I think the three of us should start having monthly adventures."

Austin's head whipped toward Luke. *Really?*

Luke shrugged. "There are a lot of cool places in Colorado that we could explore—together."

Mom sat on the arm of Luke's chair. "Well, Grace, I guess your plan worked."

Austin's attention snapped Grandma's way. "What plan?" *Now what are they talking about?*

"Let me guess." Luke's eyes narrowed as he looked at Grandma. "You concocted this whole trip to get the three of us to spend more time together."

Grandma's thin shoulder rose. "Well, I admit it was one of the reasons. You used to all be so close. I was hoping this trip would draw you together again."

Celia reached out to squeeze Grandma's hand. "Here I thought it was your plan to get us to stop using our phones so much."

Grandma gave a wry little smile. "That was another reason. I hoped you would have such a wonderful time exploring nature that you would put down your devices once in a while. I had no idea you would lock them up for half the trip."

Tricky lady. "I just assumed you wanted to see if those old trinkets were still where you had left them all those years ago."

Grandma's gaze traveled around the room before she answered. "Well, that certainly was part of it as well. But I haven't been completely honest about this trip."

Austin squeezed his eyes shut. *Please, no bad news.* "Story time."

His eyes flew open to see Grandma's eyes crinkle with laughter.

She took a deep breath, then continued. "Long ago, a few months before our trip to the Southwest, Harry and I had an experience that changed our lives forever."

The whole family stared in rapt attention.

"As you know, our father was an archeologist. One day, he received a phone call from a colleague who wanted him to travel to Missouri to check out a new discovery. My mother was out of town, so Harry and I accompanied him." She settled back against her pillow. "While we were helping our father catalog items, we came across an object that seemed almost miraculous."

No one dared move, afraid to interrupt the story.

"Harry and I have discussed the event many times over the years. We both believe the item was a relic."

"You mean, it was something that belonged to a saint?" asked Dad.

Grandma nodded. "The event was so astounding that it solidified my faith and eventually led Harry to become a monk. In fact, his abbey, in Atchison, is near where the event occurred."

Austin let out the breath he'd been holding. "Sounds amazing." *Imagine finding an item that had actually belonged to a saint.*

Grandma smiled. "Yes, it's a fascinating story. But one for another day. While Harry and I have often discussed the event, after that day we didn't really talk about it with our father. But apparently, it had an amazing effect on him as well. You see, when we recently came across our father's journal, we discovered that he also believed the item was a relic. He became obsessed with the thought of precious relics that had disappeared. Harry and I never knew it, but after that event, our father began helping the Church track down lost relics. It turns out, some of our summer excursions were part of that mission."

Austin leaned close. "So, he really was like Indiana Jones."

"I suppose he was." Grandma clasped her hands together. "The journal also revealed that there were several cases that he had never been able to solve. One occurred during our Southwest trip. He wrote about a meeting he had during our trip, with a man who had many old pieces that had been stolen from a priest in the late 1800s. The priest was making his way to visit the newly opened churches in the Southwest, bringing them gifts of relics from other parishes. But the West, at that time, was called wild for a reason. The train he was travelling on was held up and the precious items stolen." Grandma paused to take a sip of water. "The relics were lost for many years. Eventually, an antique dealer came across some unusual items at an estate sale. The man recognized the trinkets as small reliquaries—containers that hold relics. He contacted the bishop, and my father was commissioned to verify the authenticity of the items."

"What happened?" Mom asked, her voice breathy.

"Well, the journal entry states that Dad did meet with the gentleman. But before he had a chance to study the items, they disappeared."

"Someone stole them?" Luke's brows furrowed.

Grandma let out a sigh. "Our father never knew what happened to them."

A thought flickered through Austin's brain. "Was that the gentleman who gave you the coins?"

Grandma's face paled. "Harry and I believe so. We didn't really remember any of this until we read the journal. Then we started piecing it together. We realized we may have inadvertently buried precious relics."

Celia sucked in breath. "Those unusual little pendants are relics?"

None of them breathed. *No way.* He actually *had* found a relic! Austin stared at his grandmother, then turned to look at Dad, whose mouth gaped open.

Grandma's trembling hand touched her mouth. "We have no idea how the relics could have gotten mixed up with the coins and useless items the man had given us, but the timing was suspicious. If we had buried them, we realized we couldn't leave them there. So, we decided the only thing we could do was to try and find out if our buried items were still where we left them."

No one spoke for a moment while the words sank in.

"And you are hoping the relics can help provide a miracle cure," Austin whispered.

"Cure?" Grandma's head tilted.

"For Harry." Time to fess up. "I overheard your conversation with him. He's sick, isn't he?"

Grandma's eyes brimmed with compassion. "Oh, Austin."

Oh no. "You're the one who's sick?" He choked out the words. He'd been trying so hard to convince himself that his first worries were unfounded.

Grandma reached for his hand. "No, darling. I'm not sick. The conversation you overheard was about the bag we'd buried at the Grand Canyon."

"There was one at the Grand Canyon?" Luke asked. "Why didn't you ask for our help?"

"It was buried at the West Rim. When you all talked about the new visitor center in that area, I began to worry. Harry called to confirm that the new tourist area was where we'd buried the bag." Grandma's eyes squeezed shut. "It is gone forever, and I can't tell you how guilty I feel."

"Is that what you were talking to the park ranger about?" Celia asked.

Grandma answered with a curt nod. "It was a long shot, but I so hoped that maybe there was some display or record of items they had found during construction."

Now it all made sense—the phone call, her strange behavior, the plea to go visit a priest. Poor Grandma.

Luke was the first to break the heavy silence. "Grandma, did you ask the park ranger about the Native American Reservation?"

Grandma's face scrunched in confusion. "I don't understand."

"The West Rim visitor center was constructed by a local tribe. They would be the ones to ask about any found items."

Grandma's eyes flicked toward Dad. "Do you think we could inquire?"

"It certainly doesn't hurt to make a few phone calls." Dad raked his hand through his hair. "But why didn't you just tell us all this from the beginning?"

She let out a sigh. "I considered telling you before the trip, and it probably would have made life a whole lot easier. In the end though, I decided that it might be best to see if the bags could actually be located first. After so many years, I wasn't sure I could find the locations or if the bags would even still be around. Since Harry was unable to take leave to travel with me, the only way I could figure out how to get to the locations to see for myself was to have you bring me. The more I thought about this trip, the more I knew it was just what your family needed—to spend quality time together. Then after seeing how much the kids enjoyed working on Operation Coin-Find, I realized they'd needed a grand adventure to bring them together." Her gaze landed on each of her grandchildren's faces. "Harry has been my closest ally throughout my life, and I wanted you kids to experience that unique sibling bond as well. You all have been searching for good, dependable friends. Maybe you don't need to look as far as you think you do because they have been right in front of you the whole time."

Celia's head cocked to the side, and Luke's brows furrowed.

Austin stared at Grandma, then looked at his siblings. "You mean *us?*"

Grandma nodded. "Siblings are a blessing from God. Not everyone has them. God cares for each family, no matter the size, and only-children have their own unique blessings and challenges, just ask your father." She flashed a quick smile toward Dad. "But those of us who are granted siblings should cherish those first and forever friends."

Huh.

As Austin contemplated the concept, the question that had been rolling around his head suddenly became a coherent thought. "Grandma, did you say there were other relics that your dad was unable to track down?"

She nodded.

"We should try to find them." He'd look good in an Indiana Jones hat.

She chuckled. "The thought is wonderful, but if my father couldn't find them, then I doubt we would have any luck."

His enthusiasm sagged. "Yeah, I guess."

"We could at least research them," Celia offered.

Luke nodded. "Maybe it will trigger another memory. And it would be a cool thing to do together."

Dad leaned over to give his mom a kiss on the cheek. "After you collapsed, I wondered if the coins were worth something. I never would've guessed just how valuable those hidden bags actually are."

Unbelievable. An actual treasure at the end of their quest.

Celia held out the bags like they might suddenly burn her. "I can't believe I've been carrying around priceless relics. No wonder you freaked when you found out we'd buried them again."

Grandma patted her chest. "Yes, that was quite the scare. I suppose I should have told you the whole story sooner, but I loved how much fun you were having together. I didn't want to change the dynamics at all."

Dad shook his head. "Well, this will certainly be a summer to remember."

What an understatement.

Grandma lifted the bags from Celia's hand. "I think you mean a summer to treasure."

Acknowledgments

The southwest region of the United States is a very special place to me. I have many treasured family memories of the various national parks of Arizona and Utah. My first experience was as a young teenager when I traveled via camper with my family and grandparents to Bryce Canyon. I was captivated from the moment I saw the spectacular park. As we pulled up, a perfect double rainbow arched across the expanse of the unique canyon, leaving us all in awe. Over the years, my husband and I took our children on numerous trips to the Southwest, from visiting the Grand Canyon with a toddler and tiny baby to our most recent road trip from New Mexico to Nevada with our adult children and son-in-law. The natural, rugged wonders of the Southwest never cease to inspire.

So, my first thank you is to God for His incredible creation, which sparked my creativity.

To my beloved "mental" family for continually blessing me with love and inspiration.

To my friends at Catholic Teen Books, especially Theresa Linden, Corinna Turner, Amanda Lauer, and Susan Peek for offering early feedback on this story.

To two incredibly talented editors, Tressa Lindsay and Janet Johnson, who continually help make my stories shine.

To Jeanie Egolf and Perpetual Light Publishing for bringing this special story to life.

To all the readers who take the time to read my creations and bless me with support.

Other Titles by Leslea Wahl

The Perfect Blindside
eXtreme Blindside
Where You Lead
Into the Spotlight
Charting the Course
In Plain Sight
To Serve and Protect
The Mommy Mix-up

Contributing author in CatholicTeenBooks anthologies:
Secrets: Visible & Invisible
Gifts: Visible & Invisible
Treasures: Visible & Invisible
Ashes: Visible & Invisible
Shadows: Visible & Invisible

Discussion Questions

1)   This story is about family relationships. Each family is unique. Some people have lots of siblings, others are only children. There are blended families, adoptive families, and foster families. No matter what your unique family looks like, it is special and an important part of who you are. What are you most grateful for when it comes to your family?

2)   Luke spent a lot of time focusing on fitting in with a certain friend group, but in the process, neglected other aspects of his life. Have you ever found yourself in a similar situation? Are there things you'd like to currently change about who you spend your time with?

3)   Celia faced a difficult situation with her two best friends. Have you lost friends because of bad decisions? If so, how did you handle it? Were you able to confide in your family? If you handled the situation like Celia and kept it to yourself, why?

4)   Austin felt frustrated that his older siblings continued to treat him as the little brother. Have you ever felt someone in your family doesn't see who you've become? Have you taken time to understand the new interests of family members?

5)   Each of the siblings tended to use their phones as an escape mechanism, turning to them when they didn't want to interact with each other. When they finally put their phones away, they were able to enjoy and truly experience their vacation. Do you feel you spend too much time on devices? Do you feel technology has an overall positive or negative role in your life?

6)   Grandma Grace had a secret that she kept from the whole family. Did you enjoy how the secret unfolded? Do you think she succeeded in helping her grandchildren reconnect? How do you think the story would have developed if she had told them the truth from the beginning?

7)   Grandma Grace offered the kids some advice throughout the story. Have you received some words of wisdom from a grandparent or parent that stays with you?

8)   If you have siblings, have you ever thought of them as your first and lifelong friends? Does this change how you view your relationships? Does it make you want to change anything?

9)   The family connected over the personal stories they shared. Do you think that was an effective way to draw them closer? Is this something you might consider implementing in your family?

10) Were you intrigued by the lost relics? Did you know that every Catholic church contains the relics of different saints? Do you know which saints' relics your church possesses? If not, make it a family project to find out and learn about that faithful servant of God.

11) Who was your favorite character, and why?

12) What is your most memorable family vacation? What made it so unique?

13) Grandma asks the kids to read Ephesians, Chapters 4 and 5. Take a few minutes to read these passages. What stands out to you? Why do you think she suggested these verses?

Dear Reader,

If you enjoyed reading A Summer to Treasure, I would appreciate it if you would help others enjoy this book too. Here are some ways you can help spread the word:

Lend it. This book is lending enabled, so please share it with a friend.

Recommend it. Help other readers find this book by recommending it to friends, family, teachers, readers' groups, book clubs, and libraries.

Share it. Let others know you've read the book by posting a note to your social media account and/or Goodreads account.

Review it. Please tell others why you like this book by reviewing it on your favorite site.

Everything you do to help others learn about my book is greatly appreciated!

Did you know? Grandma has a backstory!

For more of Grace's childhood adventures, check out the following short stories which appear in the CatholicTeen-Books.com anthologies *Treasures: Visible & Invisible* and *Shadows: Visible & Invisible*.

"Grace Among Gangsters"
When threatened by mobsters, Grace receives help from a surprising source.

"Grace and the Grave Robber"
Grace doesn't know what it means to go "souling," but she certainly wasn't expecting it to be like this!

About the Author

Leslea Wahl lives with her family in beautiful Colorado. She strives to write Young Adult and Middle Grade novels that encourage teens to grow in their faith through fun, adventurous mysteries. Visit Leslea's website at www. LesleaWahl.com